**RANT**

Alfie Crow was born in Wallsend, Northumberland and now lives in Thirsk, North Yorkshire. He studied Drama and English Literature at Bangor University in North Wales, and studied for a PhD in Drama at Bristol University in North Somerset. He likes using the word North. He worked for many years in community theatre, writing and directing over thirty plays, as a college and university lecturer and as a poet coach in primary and secondary schools. Alfie was one of the winners of the Bridport prize in 2006 for his short story, Metal, and works as a performance poet, his poems having been published in many periodicals and collections. Rant is the first in a series of novels featuring the world's worst spy and disgruntled jobbing actor, Mike Rant. C[illegible] ed to join the secret service using [illegible] iberty to divulge th[illegible]

# RANT

ALFIE CROW

First Published 2013 by Moth Publishing an imprint of Business Education Publishers Limited.

Paperback ISBN 978 1 901888 88 1 Ebook ISBN 978 1 901888 92 8



A CIP catalogue record for this book is available from the British Library.

Cover design by **courage**.

Printed and bound in Great Britain by Martins the Printers Ltd.

Moth Publishing
Chase House
Rainton Bridge
Tyne and Wear
DH4 5RA

www.mothpublishing.com

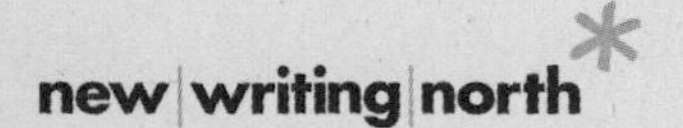

For Kate Fox,
for being so wonderful,
for being there,
for being.
Your turn now little fox.
Alfie

# PROLOGUE

Before we start, I would like to make a short statement.

I often find, however, that it is not in my nature to make short statements.

I have been called excitable, voluble, a pain in the arse and many other things, but never abrupt, short or to the point.

But I'll try.

Here goes.

The events here depicted now seem firmly consigned to the past, but they are of course vital to my own history and, I think you will agree, to the history of our fair country. It is the burden of those of us involved in the underbelly of politics and world events that we are seldom, if ever, allowed to tell our version of events. More recently the tide of human life has carried me to some surprising and really quite bizarre places, and these will be dealt with in due course. But every story must start somewhere, and mine starts here. (Well, I say here – obviously it didn't *start* here, but this is where the main narrative thrust of my life begins. The juicy bits. The money shot. Oh, how apt that phrase is…)

Anyway. Just let me explain.

Whilst the following story is completely true, I have slightly changed my own identity. Partly to make myself seem more pleasant to the fairer sex among my readership but also to avoid prosecution and/or violent death, or, at the very least, a good kicking. I have tried to make a faithful record of events as they occurred and to give a good impression of how I felt at the time. Though short of standing over you with a gun and shouting, 'Quick the police are coming and they're going to hold you responsible for all the evil deeds in the universe', I'm not sure that's possible. Not that any of the events contained herein were my fault – or at least none of the important ones. Or only some of them.

Unless you include obtaining money under false pretences.

Or the borrowing of various motor vehicles without permission.

Or perverting the course of justice.

And, of course, the use of sarcasm and choice language in a built-up area.

Oh, and being party to the kidnapping of several young people with multiple disabilities, though that was definitely just a case of being caught up in the excitement of the moment. Going with the flow.

And the same could really be said about all the explosions, the arson, the molesting of various Indigents and the so-called high treason charge that in my opinion was trumped up because none of the other stuff was going to stick in court.

Or the thing about interfering with the dead guy. But I was desperate at the time.

That came out all wrong.

No, wait, if you'd just let me explain…

# ACT I
# **THE CORPSE**

## SCENE ONE
## FEET OF FLAMES

*Wednesday May 5th. Not long after midnight.*

Where was I?

Oh yes, there I am, liberally splashing paraffin around the living room of my ex-best friend, paying special attention to the armchair in the centre of the room, and its occupant. He looks somewhat the worse for wear and I can't say I'm surprised. I think I'd look pretty shit if I'd been through, etc. etc.

Next, into the hallway, the kitchen, and finally the bedrooms. I half-heartedly wipe away fingerprints as I go. There isn't really enough paraffin for the bathroom too, but to be honest I'm hoping it won't matter too much. I'm kind of new to this game but, like everyone else in the western hemisphere, I've seen enough daytime/real-crime TV to kid myself I can dispose of sufficient forensic evidence to keep them guessing. Buying time. Also, I've appeared in a couple of episodes of *Crimewatch* and believe me it's amazing the titbits you can earwig in that particular studio. Can't wait to see the next episode, where some smooth presenter tries to explain to a perplexed public that: *The man seen in this reconstruction is wanted for questioning by the police – not for the crime he's reconstructing, but for another crime, which will be reconstructed by someone else, who is not wanted for questioning. Not yet, anyway. Except possibly by his agent who wants to know why she wasn't told he'd found some work and wants to know where her ten percent is.*

Anyway, my paraffin tin runneth empty now and there's no time to stand around philosophising, so I make my way back to the living room to confront my friend. He hasn't moved, which is something of a relief, but the smell in here is appalling. The fumes – and something else. Not his fault but decidedly unpleasant. I pull my balaclava down over my mouth and suck air through the damp wool, still soaked from my earlier outing.

'Thorry about thith,' I mutter, and try to find some kind of meaning in his gaze. But there's nothing; just the empty eyes of one already gone before. I sigh, pull out the gun and aim it between his eyes.

I squeeze the trigger.

I sigh again and spend a couple of seconds trying to figure out where the safety is. I give a lever a hopeful tweak, take aim, and before you can say, *bang, you're dead;* I've shot him twice in the head.

Bad idea!

I have had more than my share of bad ideas in the last couple of days, but this really is the cherry on top of the fucking cake.

I am so appalled and distracted by the mess his head makes as it explodes that I only vaguely take note of the spark that drifts from the barrel of the gun and lands daintily on the carpet by the chair. Suddenly, with a *wooff*, the headless chairman disappears in a fireball and the flames spread out across the carpet like, well, like flames across a paraffin-soaked carpet.

Desperately I grab my bag, and find it alight. I am very well aware that the whole room is now on fire, thank you very much, and that only my soaking clothes have saved me from instant flash-frying. I dive out the door and slam it behind me, only to hear the *whooosh* of it going up in flames as I dart into the kitchen and hurriedly douse the bag among the dishes soaking in the sink. I run for the door and get halfway through before the kitchen explodes and the blast blows me halfway down the garden.

I gingerly pick myself up, steaming gently, and stagger the rest of the way to the road. I look around to see if anyone is watching; of course, every curtain within a hundred yard radius is twitching manically. But so am I, so who am I to talk? Time to take my bow and leave. My first paid starring role, my first lead – and almost certainly my last.

In the distance, sirens. I rapidly fumble my keys out of my pocket and onto the ground where, as I bend to pick them up, I notice that my shoes are on fire.

(I'm sure that before you read this you'll have seen it, recorded by the ever-present CCTV's of Olde London Town, now become public property. The footage of me, Britain's premier cold-blooded assassin, bankrobber and flower stealer, dancing a jig up and down the gutter puddles like some manic Gene Kelly.

Michael Flatley, eat your heart out.)

I eventually climb into the car, my shoes still smouldering gently, and catch the eyes watching me nervously from the back seat as I begin to make my getaway.

Correction – I *continue* to make my getaway.

Correction again – I CONTINUE MY BRAVE QUEST TO CLEAR MY SULLIED NAME IN THE FACE OF AN UNCARING WORLD LOOKING FOR A SCAPEGOAT.

There, that feels better.

I'm in your average North London estate and I can only hope my driving is as random as it feels. Hard right, straight on, hard left, hard right, hard right, hard right—hey, I've been here before, flat's still burning nicely, I note. I have no idea where I'm going, but thankfully nor do the emergency services. After a while, having passed the same fire crew and ambulance for at least the third time, and having been stopped by a policeman on a mountain bike for directions to the house I've just left (luckily he doesn't notice my backseat passenger), things quieten down and I find myself on some anonymous A road going north.

Time for a little quiet reflection.

We have a little time. For me it would seem to be borrowed – for you, I don't know. Maybe you're reading this to relax and take your mind off the fact that you're being pursued by faceless gangsters, the police, and possibly the secret services of some of the most powerful countries in the world. I think not, however, so you're going to have to trust me on how that feels.

All will become clear, if you will just let me explain.

Please allow me to introduce myself; I'm a man of wealth and taste. Ha-de-fucking-ha. Wealth I have by the carrier bag-full, taste – well, you only have to turn on your TV and there I'll be, entertaining the nation, wearing the latest in haute couture dosser's outfits.

My name is Mike Rant (born Michael Grant) and I used to be an actor. I know, I know, sounds a bit too like *My name is Mike Rant and I used to be an alcoholic.* I took the stage name Mike Rant because I thought it sounded edgy – that it had a bit of attitude – perfect for all those gritty, Mockney, ten-a-penny gangsta movies that Brit cinema seemed to be churning out every other week. Unfortunately it also sounds a bit like "migrant", as in "worker". Those dispossessed souls who wander the earth in search of a crust. And that seems to be what I have become.

I am thirty-three. This is probably not significant other than for the fact that I should really know better, and that thirty-four seems only a distant possibility.

I live (lived?) with my wife (ex-wife? late wife?) on a featureless, sprawling estate just outside of Newcastle, which really could have been plonked down anywhere in the country and you wouldn't notice the difference, except maybe the accent of the people in the corner shop would have changed. And the local news reports might feature dramatic reconstructions of Scousers who had almost gone on holiday to Turkey the week the earthquake happened instead of Geordies.

I am on the run. The police wish to question me about the murder of my wife and are eager to know the whereabouts of her body. Also I have purloined some cash and kidnapped a law-abiding senior citizen of the portly, North American variety who is squashed into the trunk of the car I have stolen, and who squeaks every time we hit a speed bump. Not to mention the shifty-looking guy on the back seat.

Could happen to anybody, I hear you say. Why not just stop and explain?

Good question. In reply, your Honour, let me just state for the record that I, Michael Eustace Grant, for various selfish reasons of my own, do not wish to be questioned by the police. I have appeared in enough episodes of *The Bill* (you may remember me as Northern Villain IV, Deaf-Mute Homeless Man II, Transvestite Body in Canal) to have an instinctive fear of those men in ill-fitting suits and dentures who wish to pass a little time with me. My view is that these are men who know that violence is not the answer, but certainly cuts out some of the boring questions.

I am also being hunted by some nameless, random group of international terrorist or security forces who have not deigned to tell me why – though it would seem that recently they offered me a great deal of money to join forces with them in killing short, fat, second-rate politicians from the Balkans.

But, I hear you ask gentle reader – *How can it be that a second-rate jobbing actor of the extra type has become such an urgent addition to the invitation list of every coppers' ball in the land?*

Well, first let me state for the record that I resent that second-rate line. I've done my time, three years hard humiliation at drama school to be exact, and my acting skills really are not that bad – not that I get to use them very much. But I work (or rather, I don't) in the *theatre* dahling, and if there's one thing that I have learnt then it is that talent has little to do with workload, and that a celebrity is just a nonentity who struck it lucky.

Bitter, *moi?* Oh yes, indeedy. I have worked under too many twenty-year-old wankers with a director's chair and private incomes, who think a subtext refers to the menu in a takeaway sandwich shop, not to feel bitter as lemons.

And yes, I have heard all the jokes: *How many actors does it take to screw in a light bulb? A hundred – one to climb the ladder and the other ninety-nine to say, 'That should have been me up there!' What do you get if you put ninety-nine lesbians and a support actor in a room? A hundred people who don't do dick. What's the difference between a jobbing actor and a bucket of shit? The bucket.* And yes, it does get you down, after two years reading the back pages of *The Stage* and wondering if it really is time to apply for that job as a topless go-go dancer (after all, the demand seems endless and I have bigger tits, a better sense of rhythm and am probably more desperate for cash and therefore more willing to whore myself out than most of the women I was at drama school with). Yes, of late I had begun to have lurid daydreams of yours truly in a spangled G-string dancing to the 'Stars-on-45' version of Abba, with big bundles of tenners bulging out from between my arse cheeks. Not pretty. The image, that is. My arse isn't all that bad.

It had gradually dawned on me that you do not go into the theatre to earn money, you go in to spend it, and you need lots before you start if you are going to build up a wide enough circle of cronies to stage anything turgid and large-scale enough to attract the attention of the critics. And don't even get me started on critics.

But this is not the reason I have become a one-man crap repository. I have not had a breakdown owing to my lack of success in the Arts and am not randomly striking back at society in a cry for help. If I wanted that kind of attention I could easily vandalise the Blue Peter Garden (and generate sympathy for my cause at the same time by distressing the smug presenters of that formidable institution – who do they think they are anyway? Barely out of drama club and already on prime time TV).

No, I explain all of this simply to show why the argument occurred, as I believe that that is where all of this began.

*Monday May 3rd. Morning.*

It wasn't the first argument of its sort, but it was a real doozy. Anna was up, dressed, breakfasted, and hurriedly finishing off a coffee before leaving to work at some shitty little solicitor's office in Newcastle by the time I staggered downstairs.

Anna, like me, trained as an actor. Anna, like me, quickly came to hate the world she had entered into. Anna, unlike me, realised that in order to live you have to have some kind of contingency plan for earning your daily crust and feeding your habits, and that it's no good sitting around whinging about it and hoping that one day you'll get up and open *The Guardian* to find that the world has surrendered and come around to your way of thinking, sorry about the delay.

So. Anna went to work each day at seven thirty and I sat around the house and cried about my life not turning out how I'd wanted it to.

Then Anna came home every day at six thirty and I dug down deep into my emotional psyche and always seemed to find the energy to cry a bit more about the fact that life didn't turn out how I'd wanted it to.

More often than I deserved, she was sympathetic. Occasionally, however, she told me to eff off, grow up, get out of the house and find some work, earn some money and eff off, as we both knew what a joke the theatre world was so it was time to cut our losses and get on with life so eff off. Or something like that. There may have been more *effs*.

So this particular Monday I came downstairs feeling that post-day-of-doing-nothing-with-nothing-but-more-of-the-same-to-look-forward-to-today blues kind of feeling. I knew that I wouldn't be able to shake most of it off until at least my second cup of tea, but the *post-* bit beckoned. I went and rummaged through the letters stacked on the hall radiator, looking for that much-delayed missive from

Kenneth Branagh. *Dearest Mike, how are you, you old bugger? Didn't have your latest address, so the new epic's been on hold for the last two years.... Please find cheque enclosed (hope it's enough to be going on with) and feel free to adjust script if you don't like it/feel you haven't got enough lines/think Helena Bonham Carter gets too much time on screen generally and someone has to make a stand. Look forward to seeing you at your convenience, dear heart – love K.B.*

It wasn't there, of course.

What was there was a bank statement from a week ago that I hadn't dared look at yet and some nonsense from *Readers Digest* telling the homeowner they're a millionaire, if they order the English Civil War Diary Collection – forty-eight volumes at the bargain, never-to-be-repeated price of forty-four pounds and seventy-three pence each. Shite.

'No post,' said Anna, between gulps of tea.

'Well, thanks for telling me,' I replied. 'That's ruined my morning now; I could have happily spent a few hours working that one out. Now what am I going to do?'

'Eff off,' came the jolly riposte, which is not to suggest that Anna is unoriginal in her arguments, but as I said, we've done this one rather too often for either of us to generate much enthusiasm.

'Ooooh! Get you!' says me. 'Someone got out of the wrong side of the calendar this morning.'

'Yes,' she screamed merrily, 'me! I seem to have ended up getting out of the side that involves working for a living yet a-effing-gain.'

'Oh, here we go,' I suggested helpfully, 'come on, let's rake all this shit up again. You suffer so much and I just—'

'No,' said Anna to me, in joyful tones as befitted the new day, 'you're the one who effing suffers. You have to wank around here all day in your own sad effing company trying to make sense of the complete waste of space that you are, well I'm sad for you, because you're not even worth…feeling…sad…at…'

I tried to find some kind of sense in all of that but we were both a bit tired, so I just asked a perfectly civil question.

'What are you on about?'

'Money,' she explained. 'As in, you have none, you better find some, you're going to pay the bills this month, you're going to pay the mortgage this month, I'm not subbing you anything this month, so you can fuck off, fuck off, fuck off, fuck off, fuck off!'

I was sure this last outburst was because she'd forgotten to intersperse her whole sentence with *eff-offs*, so she had to squeeze them in at the end. But it was unlike her to actually say it, and some dim part of my brain began to fathom that she might actually be really upset. It makes for awkward reading on the page, but it's quite impressive if you read it aloud to yourself; especially on the bus.

'Oh, come on,' I whined, in my best Bruce Willis whiny voice, 'don't be like that...'

But Anna had had enough and she strode past me, slamming the front door behind her hard enough to rattle my fillings. (Mind you, some of them are so shit the slightest draught can rattle them.)

I sat trying to think of some witty line to throw at her but nothing came. Still, that doesn't usually stop me so I jumped up and flung the door open again.

'You know what you are, don't you?' I screamed.

But I'd left it too long, as usual, and Anna had disappeared down the cut. All that was there was a little old man whose poodle was shitting at the bottom of our drive. He looked a bit shifty and then slipped his hand inside a Marks and Spencer carrier bag to cup under the dog's bottom as it pooped. The dog looked terribly confused, if not overly unhappy at the arrangement – the old guy just looked as if he was about to throw up his porridge.

I watched for a few seconds, genuinely fascinated in spite of myself, then harrumphed loudly and slammed the door as hard as I could, hoping Anna was still within hearing distance and would feel terrible remorse that she had lowered me to this.

As the door slammed there was a crack and a slight tinkle, followed by a shriek and a yelp. Wondering how the art of slamming doors without physical damage has remained a feminine art, I opened the door again sheepishly, but couldn't see any sign of damage. I was distracted by a yelping sound and looked round to see the old guy shuffling down the street, occasionally looking daggers in my direction, in pursuit of the poodle which looked to have a Marks and Spencer carrier bag sticking out of its arse.

I slammed the door again, but the moment was gone and my heart really wasn't in it so it just closed with a bit of a dull thud that nobody except me would really notice; my life in a nutshell.

I decided to make some tea.

Then I got to thinking that maybe I should have a shit first.

*Or* I could make a cup of tea and sit on the toilet with it – now we're talking! And what about some toast and that last scrape of Marmite I hid…

Just then a shadow crossed the hall and the doorbell went. Finding a direction for the day at last I rattled open the door, ready to launch back into it with Anna.

'Ha!' I shouted triumphantly, if a little unoriginally, and the motorcycle courier on the doorstep hurriedly stepped back and stared at me threateningly.

After a moment he mumbled something through his helmet at me. It sounded like, 'Are you Number Six?'

'I am not a number, I am a free man!' I mumbled back. The little I could see of his face managed to look both confused and pissed-off (perhaps he was a fellow resting thespian, given the range of emotions at his fingertips), so I signed for the proffered package and sent him on his way.

*Bulky parcel,* I thought, *scripts, by the feel of it.* Perhaps my agent had finally pulled her finger out of her bottom (or someone else's) and got me some work for a change – or should that be for some small change.

You'll have to pardon the fact that I didn't get terribly excited at the prospect, but I knew what kind of work it was likely to be. I'd probably flick through four hundred pages of script to find one line highlighted.

*The crowd murmurs excitedly/angrily/happily (Delete as appropriate)* or *The crowd laughs, cheers, then moves forward hungrily, menacingly as Tess knocks a coconut from the shy,* or, if the Gods are truly smiling, there might even be a speaking part – *16th peasant: Please sir, we are but poor men…*

Amazing how often that one crops up; the seventeenth-, eighteenth- and nineteenth-century equivalent of *Can I interest you in a* Big Issue, *sir, madam?*

I dropped the parcel onto the kitchen table, opting for a bit of deferred gratification. Time for such fripperies later, I kidded myself. Or rather I didn't.

In the meantime, I

made some tea and found there was no milk;

made some toast and found there was no margarine;

consumed both on the toilet and then found there was no toilet roll;

washed myself, and the crockery, in the bathroom sink (yes of course I changed the water in between, what kind of animal do you think I am?) and retreated once more into the kitchen.

I looked at the parcel and then the clock.

Then I thought *Bollocks, still six hours to 'Countdown'.*

And I opened it.

My first response was to laugh. This had to be a joke, and one in fairly poor taste.

What I'd removed, thinking it was some weirdly formatted script, was in fact a bundle of cash.

Lots and lots of cash.

I stared at it, thinking that someone went to a lot of trouble to photocopy this, cut it up and bundle it into an envelope. Not to mention sending it over by courier. But the problem was it looked quite real.

Very real.

Big fat healthy bundles of English fifty-pound notes wallowing on the table.

It had to be a send-up. I emptied out the rest of the contents of the envelope, looking for some kind of explanatory note, but there was only a very large handgun of some description, some bullets, and a map.

I say "only", but for some strange reason the sight of these objects caused me to leap from my chair and run out into the garden holding onto my pants like a four-year-old who desperately needs to pee. I became aware of the fact that I was running around in very small circles and hyperventilating. Then I also became aware of an old lady with one of those Zimmer-frame-cum-shopping-trolley things watching me concernedly from the road.

'Alright?' I said. 'I…er…I'm alright. Just burned my hand. On the gun—no! On the toaster.'

She watched for a moment longer and then wandered on her way, muttering something about *bloody nutters, wasn't like that in her day, people had the manners to be mad in their own bloody houses.* Or something. Perhaps I was just a bit stressed and projecting.

Worried at who else might be watching, I strode purposefully up toward the house, tripped, and fell flat on my face. Swearing my way rapidly through the *Webster's Concise Encyclopedia of Rude Sayings and Expletives*, I looked down to see what I'd fallen over.

It was a number two.

By this I do not mean to suggest that Mr Poodle Molester had been remiss in his poop-collecting duties; it was an actual number two. The actual number two from our front door. The actual number two, which I had heard falling off during my door-slamming extravaganza earlier in the day.

I looked at the front door. The number six was still there but not the two. My brain clunked and heaved and suddenly everything fell into place as rapidly as I had hit the front path.

*Are you No. 6?*

Of course! Everything was all right with the world. See, I live on one of those weird new estates where there is only one street, and it winds back and forth quite randomly. At the end of the road are Nos. 2 and 4, then there is an unmarked cul-de-sac containing all the houses between No. 4 and our own house, No. 26.

So the gun and the money were obviously not intended for me but for whichever homicidal maniac lived at No. 6.

Phew! Maybe I could just pop round there and say *I bet you've been waiting for this! Do let me know if you need any extra bullets won't you? No, no problem, happens all the time. Bye!*

Bugger.

I crept back into the house, half expecting a gunman to have crawled out of the envelope to join his gun, just waiting to blow me out of my unemployed (sorry, *resting*) socks. Or at least hoping that it might all have disappeared and been a figment of my overheated imagination. But everything was still there, exactly as I'd left it.

Shite.

I gingerly picked up the envelope and read the address. Yup. No. 6. No name, surprise, surprise. No name for the courier company either and I was buggered if I could remember any kind of logo on the rider.

I looked at the pile of money again and the words *police, The Bill, bills, mortgage, Anna, lie, violent death, lots of cash, naughty boy, hide, run away, organized crime, very violent death* and *cup of tea* flashed through my head with dizzying speed.

*Cup of tea* sifted itself to the top of the pile and I picked up one of the fifty-pound notes and popped round the shop to buy some milk.

Now, if you think stealing a huge wedge of cash, or contemplating using a handgun in order to somehow earn it, are sinful forms of behaviour, you should try buying a bottle of milk at your local corner shop with a fifty-pound note first thing in the morning. Talk about criminal.

After every person in the shop and every member of their extended families had scratched, sniffed and squinted at it, the guy behind the counter eventually gave me my change in pound coins and fifty pence pieces, all the while telling me I'd cleared him out of coinage for the day.

I was still fuming (and limping, from the weight of coins in my left trouser pocket) when I got home, and briefly flirted with the idea of taking the gun out and shooting the shopkeeper, to give him something to really moan about. But there are enough shopkeeper martyrs out there already without making things worse. So I made a cup of tea and sat down, trying to decide what to do.

Nothing came to me immediately, so after my third cup of tea I decided to count the money. That took a little while, what with all the change from the corner shop, but it eventually came out at fifty thousand pounds.

Less sixty-four pence for the milk.

A lot of money for a bottle of milk, sixty-four pence.

And fifty thousand pounds? Even more money.

But not my money.

Whose money?

Didn't know.

Did they know about me?

Probably not.

As far as anyone knew at that point the money has been delivered, so the only person with a problem was the guy at No. 6.

At present, I also lived in a house that had No. 6 on the door.

Ten minutes later, having fixed the number two back onto my door (see, I'd already started learning to cover my tracks) I was back at the table looking at the map.

It took a bit of searching through my old atlas to find that it was a map of the Yucatan Peninsula, with a cross drawn on it, apparently in the middle of nowhere. The nearest town of any size is a place called Tizimin, or something. Doesn't ring any bells? No, didn't for me either.

I looked at the money again. All forty-nine thousand, nine

hundred and ninety-nine pounds and thirty-six pence of it.

An awful lot of money.

Why couldn't it be my money?

Because it belonged to someone else.

Well, whose was it?

Possession being nine-tenths of the law and all that.

Presumably it belonged, until quite recently, to some Mexican group, hence the map.

Could they know about me?

Almost certainly not.

If they questioned the courier, would he tell them he brought it here?

Possibly.

Could be, he'd just say he definitely delivered the package to number six.

What if they brought him round here and he pointed out the house? Would they believe me if I said *What? What package? Be off with you, you varmints, we've had no packages here!*

Or maybe, *Please sir, we are but poor men…*

I thought not.

I started to rationalize (which is always the top of the slippery slope for me) that maybe I should have a look at whoever lives at No. 6 before I decided anything. It wasn't far away and the gardens weren't too difficult to get into, so maybe a peek through a window or two wouldn't hurt. Best to wait until nightfall though.

See? See how easy it is to fall into criminal ways of thinking? Or maybe I'm just too skilled in the dramatic arts. A human chameleon who takes on roles like other people slip into their underpants.

I'm ashamed to say that it is only at his point in my thinking that the police seriously entered into my considerations, and only then because the thought of breaking and entering and getting caught became a possibility.

'Should I go to the police?' I thought out loud, frightening myself by talking louder than I'd intended.

I decided to pass the time until darkness by making a list.

Point one: Would the police believe my story about the package being wrongly delivered? Or did having a gun and fifty thousand pounds in used notes in the house look just a little suspicious? Would they take me for a sad, dangerous lunatic? I could count on many of my friends to corroborate this, not to mention Mr Poodleman and Ms Zimmerlady, among many others.

Point two: Would they take me seriously at all? Especially if Mr No. 6 plausibly denied any involvement, which led me to—

Point three: Would drawing attention to myself only make me an obvious target for revenge with whoever the money used to belong to i.e. the Faceless, Unidentified, Nameless, Yucatan Group for the Execution of Terror (or the FUNYGETs, for short)?

Point four: Would I have to pay back the sixty-four pence that I spent on milk? (That's the kind of petty thing that really puts my back up when you try to play the Good Samaritan – it's always us honest types that end up worse off than the villains.)

Point five: What if the police are involved, or are being monitored in some way by the FUNYGETs?

Point six: I'd really, really, *really* like to keep this money, and I know that whatever happens the police will take it off me if I give them the faintest inkling that it is here.

Okay, so I decided wrong.

So sue me.

I decided to have a look at Mr No. 6 and see if I could figure out what he was up to. I decided to put the money somewhere safe until I decided what to do. And I decided I didn't dare tell Anna an effing thing, until I'd decided on the proper course of action.

As the scat singer might have said, *Bad idea, bad idea, oooh bad idea.*

## SCENE TWO
## OOPS, I DID IT AGAIN

*Wednesday May 5th. Early.*

At least my tongue feels better.

I've been driving for a couple of hours now, mulling it all over, without paying much attention to where I've been going. Bad idea. I'm a fugitive now and must start paying attention to the little things – like keeping myself alive long enough to exact a hideous revenge and live a life of luxury with my ill-gotten gains.

Besides, this is how accidents happen – and as if to prove the point, I now find myself approaching Birmingham.

The still, pre-dawn darkness, combined with the cold and my proximity to Birmingham, depresses me. Never in my life have I felt so humiliated by my own actions, so hunted, so lacking in hope for any kind of worthwhile future. And this from a man who has worked in youth theatre.

I briefly toy with the idea of spending the rest of my life driving around the stringy bit of phlegm that is Spaghetti Junction, stopping only occasionally for petrol and chilled pasties made from chicken lips and pigs' bums. No one would ever find me here. And if they did they wouldn't care. I'd have been punished enough. My latest acquisition, my newest passenger, stares at me balefully from the back seat.

I spot a garage and decide to pull over and find some fuel. And some kind of burn cream if they sell it; my face feels tight as a drum after my earlier fiasco. Getting to the garage involves swerving across three lanes of fast moving, honking, irate traffic (where are all these bastards going at four in the morning? Surely they can't all be fugitives – unless they're fleeing Birmingham, of course), but this is as nothing to an international man of mystery like my good self.

Still shaking from the several near misses (do the back of *your* knees sweat when you're scared?), I fill up the petrol tank and go in to pay. The guy behind the counter looks at me with open interest as I pay for the petrol, three pasties, two tins of travel sweets (Old-Fashioned flavour, whatever that is) and three tubes of *Soothing Ointment – Good for Haemorrhoids*. (You never know, I may be driving for some time yet.)

As he rattles noisily in the till he asks, 'What happened to yorr oibraws then, mayte?'

I desperately try not to think of the Brummie pig from the *Pipkins* puppet show as I squint into the darkened window at my reflection and see that most of my eyebrows have in fact disappeared. *The fire.* I rack my brains trying to think of a plausible explanation and the only one that pops out is:

'Canther. I have canther. Had. Cancer.'

'Bloody 'ell, cancer ov thee oibraws? Oi've never 'urd ov that, loik.'

'No, it was the, er, chemotherapy. Made my hair fall out.'

'Woi 'uv yow still gut 'air un yorr 'ead then?'

'Well, it's a bit hit and miss really. Not all of your hair falls out at once. You should see my pubes – like a Mohican they are, and my legs – hairy right down the back and bald on front.' I'm rambling now, obviously, and hope he doesn't ask me to remove my trousers and underpants. If he does I may have to shoot one of us. To be honest I would be my preferred choice.

But instead he looks at me blankly and asks, 'Ah yow taykin' tha piss?'

Astute man. Wasted in a job like this. Come on, Mike, stop being a snob.

'No,' I sigh, 'See, that's the reaction I always get. That's why I prefer only going out at night. Since...since...my mother...'

He looks ready to burst into tears. 'Hey, look, orlroyt, it's orlroyt. Sorry Oi asked. Here, tayk anuther tin uv swayts. Gow on. Yow tayk care naw. Boy, boy.'

Well, that worked, but I really must stop drawing attention to myself.

I get back behind the wheel and drum my fingers on it.

I could go into Birmingham. Ha, ha, ha. Why?

South to Bristol?

North to Manchester?

No. No good. I can't decide. I get out of the car again and open the boot.

'Manchethter or Brithtol?' I ask. 'Sorry, Brissstol.'

Silence.

'Well, what about Birmingham?' Definite shake of the head there.

'Yeah, I agree. Well?'

'Miffmuff,' comes the reply, after a second or two.

'Your people are there?'

A hesitant nod.

'Is that who you phoned last night?'

Another nod.

'Good. And when we get there, I think we'd better change cars, don't you agree?'

Again, a nod. I wonder if I should sit him in the back window to entertain passing children and lorry drivers.

'Will you help me steal one?'

Nothing.

'I'll let you sit on the back seat for a bit.'

He nods. Boy does he nod. I slam the boot, just to remind him who's boss, and see the garage attendant staring at me suspiciously. I wave and he gets busy with the chewing gum displays. I wonder how much he'll get for selling the cassette from the CCTVs on the forecourt, once he realises who I am. Weird. Ten years as an actor and I'll be on TV more in the next forty-eight hours than I could have hoped for in a lifetime.

Still, I'm feeling a bit perkier now and climb back behind the wheel for the drive to Miffmuff. Put the radio on. The Clash, singing,

*My Daddy was a bank-robber*
*But he never hurt nobody*

Yeah, and who's going to believe that?

*Monday May 3rd – Tuesday May 4th.*

On the day after my unusual delivery, I was standing in line at the bank. It was a long line, as usual. I had a rather bulky carrier bag in my hand and I was wearing a somewhat obvious false moustache and glasses. I was also very nervous. Sweaty, in fact, and sure that I'd been followed, though I can't say I'd seen any evidence to back up my paranoia.

The previous evening, having apologised for my mood that morning and made things up with Anna a bit, I told her that I'd had a phone call about some film work. It was art house stuff, by an independent director who'd got my name from a friend of a friend. Best to have some excuse for having money handy, just in case.

Art house is fairly safe as a porky pie, because that kind of stuff never gets shown in cinemas – it just seems to be a self-fulfilling prophecy of the I-told-you-the-world-wasn't-ready-to-understand-my-work kind. The fact that most of it is incomprehensible shit seems by the by to the producers.

Anna seemed a bit sceptical at first, but I managed to calm her fears with a lot of *I probably won't get it anyways* and moaning about how it was just some rich kid's fantasy that we all should suffer for his art.

She was much more suspicious when I offered to walk down to the shop and buy toilet rolls and margarine, and maybe pick up a takeaway, but that soon disappeared when I remembered to ask her for the money.

I phoned ahead to the Indian restaurant and, pulling on a black hat and jacket, I left the house and wandered down the road past the cul-de-sac, then doubled back and ran, hunched over, up the path to No. 6. Yes, I know, if anything is guaranteed to draw attention to yourself, it's behaving like a member of the SAS in suburban Newcastle, but I was nervous, all right? I crouched by the gate into the garden, doing some breathing exercises I'd picked up at a weekend workshop with the RSC, but it didn't quite work and I ended up sounding like Rolf Harris remixed by Fatboy Slim.

I had walked past the house a few times during the afternoon and it didn't look like the garden would be hard to get into. There was no sign of activity in the house and I wondered if anyone lived there or if it was just some kind of drop-off point.

One more deep breath, then I lunged over the gate, caught a bootlace on the catch at the top and crashed upside down into the other side of the door. I hung there powerless as I felt my shoelace come slowly undone, until I dropped and smacked my head on the concrete below. The first few lines of 'Starry, Starry Night' flashed though my head.

I lay still for a few seconds, not entirely through choice, to see if anyone had overheard me, but it was hard to tell through the ringing in my ears. I reached up a hand to my aching forehead and it came away covered in blood. Great.

I staggered to my feet and leant against the wall until the sickness passed, then moved on down the garden. A perfectly ordinary, suburban garden. I'm not sure exactly what I'd expected – a Sherman tank perhaps, or a Cruise missile silo; a few weapons of mass destruction painted with the Al Qaeda corporate logo, at least – but this was not obviously the garden of a killer. The lawn was a bit hummocky, though, and the hairs on the back of my neck prickled as I wondered whether this was where he buried his victims. Shaking off the thought, I moved on.

Around at the back of the house there were French windows

looking into the lounge, same as our house. The curtains were open slightly and light spilled into the garden. I squinted into the room. There was a fairly tatty three-piece suite and a lovely new widescreen TV showing one of those heart-warming documentaries about disability. Or at least it showed two massively overweight ladies, who were obviously incapable of undressing themselves, helping each other out of their clothes and washing each other in a sink before shaving each other's bikini lines. Not that I watched for very long. That was just the impression I got. Honest.

There was no sign of anyone in the room, so I moved around to the far side of the house and the kitchen. I squatted beneath the open window and peeped in.

A fairly portly man in the most enormous pair of underpants I've ever seen in my life was making himself some tea and toast. He had an enormous jar of Marmite on the bench too. Flash git. He wore an appallingly bad toupee, which appeared to be on back to front, and some enormous slippers with a stars-and-stripes motif on them. He was standing with his back to me – and what a back it was. Across his back was a series of puckered, star-shaped scars that if I didn't know any better I would have said were bullet holes. And, as I don't know any better, then I'll say they were bullet holes. Ouch. This was obviously one mean dude.

But when he turned to put some dishes into the sink I saw what looked like a perfectly ordinary, late-middle-aged man, making some supper before settling down to watch some fairly tame pornography. Nothing odd here. If you like that sort of thing, of course.

He picked up his supper and shuffled back in the direction of the lounge, whistling something I couldn't quite catch under his breath. I was still squatting there, wondering what on earth I was doing, when

I heard the lock click on the French doors. After a few seconds a voice called out, tentatively, 'Hi! Who's that out there?'

He had an American accent. I had a vision of him withdrawing a bazooka from those XXL Y-fronts (if you'll pardon the image) and advancing slowly toward me with it clutched in his hand.

'You better answer me,' he said. 'I have a gun and the police are on their way.'

Needless to say I didn't answer, and had tensed up so much I couldn't have spoken if I wanted to. Not without peeing myself, anyway. When I heard him shuffling toward me around the corner of the house I stood up quickly and I swear I heard my bladder squeak in protest. I may have done a little fart.

As he rounded the corner I leapt at him.

Actually, that's not strictly true. As he rounded the corner I tried to surprise him and run past, but my loose lace caught around my shins and as he and the path were the same width I ended up leaping onto him, while we both shrieked in terror and he fell over backwards. I skinned my knuckles too. They were really sore.

While I lay on top of him, nose-to-nose, he grabbed at my shoulders, and asked, not unreasonably under the circumstances, 'What the *hell*—hey, aren't you the guy who's been walking up and down watching my house all day? You some kind of burglar? You better speak to me right now and…and…. What…what the hell is that funky smell, boy?'

But I chose that second of distraction to give him a first-degree Chinese burn and he yelped, letting me go momentarily. I was up and off him in a flash (well, under a minute, anyway – he was a lot stronger than he looked), shouting, 'Stay where you are, you bastard, my mates are just around the corner, and if you move they'll be round here like a shot, just you see…and I've got your gun and…look, just…stay!' I could hear him struggling to get to his feet and shouting, 'Gun? What gun are you talking about?' but I had whipped open the back gate (shite, it wasn't locked after all) and run off into the night before he appeared. I ran for a few hundred yards more until my bladder got the better of me and I had to pop off behind a bush and make a noise of the horse-and-tin-bucket variety, while I got my breath back.

An American? Well, possibly. He could be putting the accent on. An American who tried to assault me? Again, possibly. It could be argued that the assaulting went the other way, I supposed. An American who was the (possible) intended recipient of a gun and large sums of money. And who very probably would be able to recognise me if he saw me again in the street or a police line-up. Or at the very least he could identify my farts. Though that was a particularly nasty one so hopefully I could get away with it if asked to repeat the process in a police line-up. And had I really told him I had his gun? Oh mercy me, what had I done?

I hurried to the Indian and picked up the takeaway, which had grown cold and congealed on the countertop. Then I popped into the corner shop and, ignoring the furious stares of the shopkeeper, picked up the margarine and toilet rolls. I had to use most of one of them to mop up the blood from my head and knuckle wounds (the toilet roll that is, not the margarine). On the way home I had time to feel a complete jerk (I didn't ask his name but he seemed to quite enjoy it, ha ha) whilst thinking up a plausible story for Anna about the group of kids who'd attempted to steal our supper and had only given up after a long hard fight which left me horribly wounded and in need of a great deal of sympathy. And kisses. Oh, and lukewarm Indian takeaway. Oh, and some of that good, hard loving. Oh, Anna.

So there I was in the bank. Bright and early. Or early, anyhow. Anna had looked even more dubious when I'd been up and out of the house before her but I didn't want to have the cash and gun hanging around the house any longer than necessary. As I'd come in some scrawny little jerk wearing a cheap suit and a rapper's attitude had sideswiped me with the door and bashed my nose. He glowered at me like I'd forced him to assault me by daring to be on the same planet as him.

As he pushed past I flailed around with my hand and somehow grabbed the tail of his coat.

He rounded on me. 'Get – your – hands – off – me!' he hissed, pulling himself up to his full five foot two.

'Well,' I said, 'I just wanted to say thank you.'

He stared at me.

'For barging the door into me,' I continued, while he continued to stare. 'Otherwise we might never have met.'

He looked a little less cocky, and his focus shifted down to my nose, obviously inspecting the damage he had inflicted. He frowned slightly. Maybe he did have some kind of conscience after all.

'I mean, it's so hard to meet people these days,' I said quietly, leaning into his face, trying to remember the lines from my last stage show. 'Since they let me out of the home. I have so few friends these days. No one to...*play* with anymore. And then you deliberately push the door into me so we can have a little...human contact. That's why you did it, wasn't it? I know how it is. I've been watching you for months now, and you've obviously been watching me too, haven't you, you cheeky little minx. It's hard to find company these days, isn't it? For people like us, who are so...*choosy* about our friends? And when

I look at you I just know we can be *gooood* friends. Can I come back to your house? I know the address, but… Do you live with anyone? Anyone who'll miss you? I – no! Come back! I love you!'

But he was gone.

People stared at me as I joined the queue, grinning to myself. They'd obviously overheard some of our conversation and were giving me some fairly searching looks until I made eye contact. Then they stared at their shoes like someone else had dressed them and they'd only just discovered how cheap and nasty they were.

'Oh lighten up,' I muttered. 'Just having a bit of fun.'

My idea (how's this for brilliant?) was to open a safe deposit box and put the cash, the map and the gun inside. I had a passport, which had been made up as a prop for an appearance in *Casualty* and which I couldn't distinguish from the real thing, so I was hoping nobody else would. The moustache I was wearing was from the same episode and matched my photograph on the passport. Whilst working at the BBC, I'd "borrowed" some headed notepaper (oh come on, everybody does it); it had only taken a few seconds to write a letter to myself, using the false name and a false address, and Robert's your mother's sister's husband, I had enough ID to carry out my plan. The huge plaster on my forehead, courtesy of my adventures the night before, helped too. I was just wondering why anybody works for a living when a life of crime and deceit is so simple, when the number light thingy changed at the front of the queue and it was my turn with the cashier.

I walked over, smiled at the bland face of the young bloke behind the counter, whose badge identified him as Norman and tried to say, in my best Lee Marvin voice, 'Good morning, I'd like to open a safe deposit box, please.'

Now, disguising your voice is one thing, but even I couldn't quite distinguish which words I'd used and whether they were in the correct order, so I wasn't at all surprised when Norman looked at me, all open-eyed, and said, 'Are you all right, sir?'

I made a great show of clearing my throat and said again, 'I'd like to open a safe deposit box. I have all of the relevant ID here.'

'Your moustache would appear to be a little...crooked, sir.'

I looked at my reflection in the countertop and saw what looked like a great hairy caterpillar crawling up the side of my nose.

'Ah!' I muttered. 'Haven't quite got used to it yet... I'm just trying it out. Have to wear it in a film next week. I'm an actor, you know.'

Norman obviously didn't know. Or care.

'Can I be of any assistance today, sir?' he said in a voice which might as well of been supplied by a ventriloquist for all the expression that showed on his face. I know I wanted to shove my fist up his arse. And not in a good way.

Sighing, I pulled off the moustache and slipped it into my pocket. *Low profile,* I reminded myself, *stealthy as a ninja.*

'I want to o-pen a safe-ty de-pos-it box, Norrrrrr-mannnn.'

'There's no need to take that tone with me. I'm not an idiot, sir.'

'Well, the chap who was here a moment ago was. Best have a word with him when you see him next.'

He handed me the forms and a tiny pen and sent me off to fill them in. After a few false starts (it's difficult sometimes to resist going onto automatic pilot and filling in the truth on those forms. Banks are so intimidating, don't you find? Or they are if you don't have any cash. Or if you do have a big bag of cash which theoretically belongs to someone else. But finders keepers and all that...) I managed to complete the form and rejoin the queue.

As luck would have it, I got Norman again – it was a fifty-fifty chance to be honest, why don't they have more bloody staff in these places – and handed over the scrawled and scribbled forms silently.

He looked at the forms and then at me like I'd just handed him a somewhat filthy love letter.

'I'll, er, need to see some identification please. Sir.'

This last sir was even more begrudged than the earlier ones. I thought about laying into his snotty attitude but for once I bit my tongue. I had to stop drawing attention to myself.

Instead, I reached into my bag and grabbed the passport and the letter, which had somehow got stuck down the side. I gave them a tug.

It went ever so quiet in the bank as the gun, dislodged from between the bundles of notes, fell with a clatter onto the countertop and lay pointing at Norman like the finger of God.

Embarrassed, I snatched it up and said; 'Look, I—let me explain—'

But my vocabulary deserted me. I guess it's just one of those situations you really don't expect to encounter and therefore you've never planned out the correct conversational gambit for it in advance.

Norman's hands had shot up into the air and he said – very calmly, I thought, given the circumstances – 'I understand, sir. Don't worry, sir, we'll take care of that for you now, sir.'

The manager (*Kathleen, Bank Customer Services Manager Level III, Hapy to Serve You,* according to her badge) noticing the sudden silence, had stepped up, holding her hands palm outward toward me, and said, 'Good morning, sir. Don't worry, sir, here at Nova Banks we're fully trained to deal with situations like this and no one is going to resist in any way. In fact I was just on a course last week and you'll be glad to know it's all fresh in my mind.' She continued as if she were reading from an autocue in front of her. 'We all want to get out of here with the least possible fuss, and without anyone being harmed—'

'No!' I shouted, amazed at how easily I could balls up a simple thing like opening an illegal bank account for some stolen money and a gun and a forged passport.

'Oh my God!' I heard someone squeak excitedly. 'He doesn't want the money, he's a thrill killer!'

I span round, gun still in my hand. 'Who said that?' I asked – a bit crossly, if I'm honest. Nobody answered, but almost every eye in the room pointed to one young woman, who was looking at the ceiling. I walked towards her. 'I suppose you think that's a clever thing to say, do you? Well you've got it all wrong, young lady. Don't you give me that attitude until you know something about me. I'm—I'm—' *I'm what?* What could I possibly say that was going to make any difference to this situation?

Luckily, Kathleen saved me. The course she'd been on really must have been quite good. I found myself wondering if they needed any actors to do role-play. With my experience…

She must have come through the connecting door silently as she suddenly appeared at my elbow smiling and simpering like a Miss World contestant who's been shown a photograph of a kitten.

'It's alright, sir, everything is under control here, sir,' she said, as all around her, her staff (and there did seem to be a lot more of them available for customer service than there were a few minutes ago) ladled handfuls of notes into cash bags, 'Follow procedure four,' she said quietly to the staff – then to me, 'No one is going to say nasty things about you, sir,' and she directed a harsh stare towards the young woman, 'or do anything to you. I would just ask everyone to remain calm and then no one will get hurt.'

I sat down on the nearest chair. How could this be happening?

'Look,' I tried again, 'I'm really not ready to walk out of here with that amount of money—'

'Oh, my God,' said the thrill-killer woman, 'He's going to hold us all hostage and kill us one by one before taking on the police. No amount of money's going to be enough. He's a suicide, I tell you, he's going for death by cop and he doesn't care who he takes with him!'

Everyone stood silently swearing. Well, not everyone. Some of them actually swore pretty loudly, given the circumstances, and Kathleen clapped her hands like a schoolmistress and said, 'Now that is quite enough from you, madam.'

I stared at the young woman.

'Do you watch a lot of TV?' I asked.

She didn't answer.

'I wasn't planning on shooting anyone,' I said quietly, 'but for you I might make an exception.'

'Please, Mr...Doolalley...?' said Kathleen, squinting at the form I'd filled in.

'Donnelly,' I corrected.

She didn't look convinced. 'Donnelly. Okay. Now, Mr Donnelly, this really is all of the money that we have to hand and everything else is locked into a time-secure vault. And killing anyone, even yourself, isn't going to change that. So I would respectfully suggest that you take what is on offer and make your getaway as best you can. And I'd like to thank you for your custom today, as every Nova Bank customer is a valued customer, no matter what their income bracket!'

She beamed at me and then turned on her heel and walked to the counter.

'Now listen,' I said, but nobody was, and nobody did. Whilst we were talking, wads of cash were being stuffed into canvas bags and then passed over the counter in my direction. When I didn't immediately go and pick them up, Kathleen herself went over and began picking them up and handing them to me. A few people from the queue even handed over the contents of their wallets, though I noticed that Miss Clever-Knickers Thrill-Killer Fantasist kept hers to herself.

I dropped the bags back onto the floor.

'Look, you don't understand,' I whinged at Kathleen, 'Let me explain—'

'Oh, I do understand, sir,' she said, 'I understand entirely. Things can be very difficult these days, sir, and there are times when it's impossible to make ends meet. But we are not here to judge. No. That is not our role. And you mustn't blame yourself, sir. But I do have to point out that my priority, insignificant as it is compared to your own priorities, I know, my priority is not to risk the lives of my staff or those of my customers, but rather to defuse the situation and make sure we all leave here safe and well, sir. With everything that we require. Within reason. So if there's nothing else...?'

She had picked up the bags again from the floor and was holding them out to me, nodding sympathetically and smiling. Just for a second, I was sure she was going to wink at me.

And at that moment, also just for the tiniest of seconds, I wanted to shoot someone. God help me, I actually wanted to shoot someone dead just to make it all stop, to make this whole nightmare stop. But instead I said, in a whisper, 'No. Thank you. Nothing else,' I glanced down at her badge, 'thank you, Kathleen. By the way, shouldn't there be two *p*s in happy?'

Before I knew what was happening I was being bundled to my feet and rushed out of the door, bags in hand, into the street. The door closed behind me with a thunk, and the bolts shot home.

Somewhere away in the distance, sirens began to wail.

'Please,' I whimpered at the heavy wood. I slumped against it, making what I can only describe as a keening sound.

The whingey ninja had struck again.

I looked down at my hands and at the three bags of money I now held where there used to be one, I looked at the gun stuffed into the waistband of my trousers, and I looked at the card Kathleen had shoved into my hand that read IF YOUR SERVICE TODAY WAS SATISFACTORY, OR IF YOU HAVE A COMPLAINT, THEN RING US ON—and I run, run, run, run, run…

## INTERLUDE 1

*Inspector Mallefant sifts through the debris halfheartedly. Looks despairingly at his feet. Another pair of brogues destined for the bin.*

*Ashes to ashes.*

*Or it would be ashes if the fire brigade hadn't reduced everything to a soggy, squelching morass of muddy filth.*

*He sighs. He's been doing that a lot recently.*

*He knows that behind his back the constables call him 'the Flying Scotsman' as he puffs and wheezes around the office. Or 'the Sighing Scotchman'. Or 'the miserable old sod with the slow puncture'. He does not care. Soon he will leave all of this behind.*

*If only it could be like the telly, he thinks to himself. Nice clean villains only too ready to confess, in nice clean houses bought from their nice clean ill-gotten gains.*

*Inspector Mallefant has been a policeman too long. He no longer yearns for the big cases, the career-makers. He does not wish to be remembered as a gritty cop who always got his man. That way filth and disorder lie. These days he dreams of nothing more than sitting out the rest of his days behind his neat, clean and orderly desk, in his spanking-clean office, in his highly polished shoes. Waiting for the clock to run down so that he can take his orderly and sterile retirement.*

*His colleagues think him a joke, a dinosaur. But he has been around too long to think he can clean up the sewer of London. It has no desire to be cleaned – and anyway, no sooner have you cleaned up a little patch than someone else is bursting to evacuate their bowels.*

*He could show you the evidence in the newspapers (if the newsprint did not come off all over his hands, a fact that had caused him to give up the* Daily Telegraph *many years before). Or on the television, those great dust magnets that hoover up the corners of every living room in the country.*

*People are obsessed with their own filth, and the filth of others. They cannot get enough of it, and they would not thank him if he were to get rid of it. So they are welcome to it.*

*Anyway, he will be off soon to sit in his highly disinfected little corner of society. Funny – people used to worry about dirt lurking in corners. Now they are terrified that some corner of cleanliness, of sanity, has escaped their clutches. They would seek it out and defile it. But not if he can help it.*

And they call us the filth, *he thinks, smiling grimly.*

*He sighs again, looking across at the young WPC, who is staring at him with a startled expression on her face. He wonders if he has been thinking out loud again (as indeed he has). Muttering about the grubbiness. The dirty, dirty, world.*

*He tries to concentrate on the matter in hand. And there does seem to be some matter on his hands. He grimaces.*

*There is little he can do until the scene-of-crime lot have finished sifting through the rubble and mud. Until some kind of identification has been made on the body. Until they've gone through all of the footage from all of the CCTVs in the area. The younger coppers hoping for something they can sell on to the TV or newspapers. Hoping for a break.*

*Now there's a thought. A nice break with a cup of tea and a sausage butty. He tries to remember if he filled his flask before he left the office.*

*'Inspector?'*

*Could these bastards read his mind? No sooner does he think of sloping off for a minute than they're after him. Wheedling. Drooling and gurgling like babies sitting in their own mess.*

*'Inspector Mallefant, sir?'*

*An off-white, ash-streaked teletubby is peeping at him around the corner of what used to be the living room. SOC woman. Sock puppet more like. He raises an eyebrow towards her.*

*'Something you should see, sir.'*

*He sighs and crosses the creaking floor, wiping his hands and his brow with his handkerchief. He pulls on a pair of rubber gloves. He would like to wear them permanently, but knows this would only draw unwanted attention.*

*The coroner is bent over the body in the chair. What's left of it, anyway.*

*Messy business. Inspector Mallefant is a neat person. A clean person.*

*When he had taken the call from Newcastle, a possible tip that a fugitive of theirs – young actor by the name of Michael Grant, a.k.a. Mike Rant – had absconded to London, he'd been happy.*

*Young actor; morally filthy, that lot, but generally clean in their habits. Gone off the rails, robbed a bank and headed for the big smoke. Spousal assault, possible homicide. Nice. Especially as the assault occurred well away from his beat. Clean-cut work. Perhaps the young man has gone a bit doolally, temporary insanity. Driven bonkers as conkers by the grubbiness of the world in which we live. Mallefant's first thoughts were pick him up, give him a spank and a confession in the bag before breakfast tomorrow. Lovely.*

*But now there's arson involved. Murder in his precinct. Kidnappings. Stolen vehicles. Soiled garments left in carrier bags. They certainly dropped this shit-pile in his lap without much warning. Who was this nutter? And who was the corpse in the lounge? Quick game of* Cluedo *before bed, was it?*

*He walks over to the coroner. Not a job he'd ever fancy, coroning, forensics, any of that gubbins. Too much rummaging around in other people's mess for his liking.*

*'Any idea who it is, then?' he asks, hopeful, but knowing that this one was never going to be that clean, that easy, that neat.*

*'Not yet,' replies the coroner, 'but we've got a fair idea who it isn't.'*

*'Don't play funny buggers, not in the mood. It's no' Grant, then?'*

*'Nope.'*

*'No' this Simon chappie, the owner, is it?'*

*'I very much doubt it, Mallefant. Off in Cannes, isn't he?'*

*'What's left of this one'll fit in a can if we try and move him. Any idea on cause of death?' His little joke, that was, stating the obvious. He gives a little dry chuckle, but not a pleasant one, like someone who doesn't chuckle often, or for the right reasons.*

*'Well, no, not really,' muses the coroner.*

*That gives Mallefant pause.*

*'What do you mean, no' really? Bugger was shot, wasn't he? Even Ah ken that, you soft shite. Look at thon hole in his heid. Could keep ma lunch in there, and Ah like a big lunch.'*

*The coroner shudders. 'He was shot, yes. That's not what killed him though, Mallefant. And it didn't do this damage either. Heat of the fire caused his brains to boil inside his skull. Sort of like a pressure cooker. Just keeps building up and building up until—'*

*'Yes, thank you, Ah ken the very lurid picture you're painting.' Mallefant sighs again. He is beginning to sound like a pressure cooker himself.* Cluedo *it is then.*

*'Smoke inhalation? His lungs went oot on him?' A shake of the head. 'The fire, burnt alive?' Shake. 'Bashed away up hes back passage with the Professor's plums?' More shaking, this time accompanied by a muffled giggle.*

*'Are you takin' the pish or what? Come on then, amaze me, O wise*

*one. How do you know it was none of they things?'*

*So the coroner tells him.*

*Mallefant doesn't answer so the coroner shows him. Proof positive, as it were.*

*And Mallefant stares at the body in front of him.*

Filthy wee beggers, *he thinks.*

## SCENE THREE
## A WALK IN THE PARK

*Wednesday May 5$^{th}$. Later, but still early.*

Running on fumes, we reach Bristol at dawn.

I stop the car, get out to stretch my legs and breathe in the air, like sucking on a damp flannel. Funny how particular places give you a particular feeling as soon as you step out of the car or off the train. I always know I'm in London because straightaway I feel in too much of a rush and get agitated, ready to barge anyone and everyone out of my way because *I'm more important and so is the pathetic little day's work I have to do*. (At the same time, you can feel the money being sucked from your pockets as you buy crap. Not just any old crap but capital crap, as in capital punishment or capital crime.) Birmingham, I instantly feel depressed and wonder when the next train out is. In Manchester I feel as though I should be a hard-hitting heroin addict getting ready to swear on primetime TV, or camping it up down Canal Street. Newcastle just feels like home, with a clippy mat on every floor and a whippet for every lap (hey, this is my list – you feel as stereotypical as you like wherever you want to feel it).

And Bristol. I step out of the car and immediately know I'm in Bristol because I'm wet. They say Bristol is one of our greenest cities and I'm not surprised, it's always bastard raining here, everything's probably covered in a fine layer of mould. I did a couple of shows here on tour and in less than a week the costumes were all covered in mildew.

But we're here; I'm still not sure about the contacts of my American friend but I am fairly short on options at the minute. I know that even if I had a plan then nothing would be going to it.

I look at the guy in the back seat.

'Are you okay?' A nod. 'Do you need to use the bottle again?' A slow, pensive shake of the head. Relief from both of us. I hope I never have to find out what it's like trying to pee in a bottle held by a man with a gun and a twitchy disposition while my hands are cuffed. Though I may use it as an exercise next time I run a drama workshop. Just as an icebreaker. 'Dealing with distraction', I could call it. Aimed at people who work in call centres. Not that I'd want them to learn anything from the experience, it would just make me feel better.

I try to find something comforting to say to my passenger but the conversation seems to have run its course, so I just scowl back at him as I get out and open the boot, waiting while Uncle Sam grimaces into the spitting rain. I help him to stand up and he looks a little wobbly, blinking in the early morning light. I ask him if he's okay and he nods distractedly, staring at the man on the back seat.

'We need another car,' I tell him.

He nods.

'Any ideas?'

He gestures towards the boot of the car. There is a small leather wallet tucked next to the spare wheel. I open it. It contains various picks and tools.

'Lock picks?' I ask. Obviously I should have searched him, I hear you say. Well I can't think of everything – it's all very well for you looking at this from the outside, Mr/Mrs/Ms Smarty Knickers (delete as appropriate).

He nods. I'm getting bored with this. I ungag him.

'Who in hellfire is that son of a bitch,' is the first thing he gasps, looking at the man on the back seat.

'Look,' I say, 'I need you to be calm right now. I'm trying very hard to be calm but my personality doesn't seem to support calm at the best of times and now is definitely just about the worstest of times I can possibly imagine and maybe that's because I'm low on imagination too but who can blame me, eh? Eh? Maybe your lot have to put up with this carry on all the time but I'm just a poor, humble, ordinary guy – well maybe not so ordinary, but the others seem to fit – and I am what you might call a tad tetchy just now. So, that being the case, can you do us both a big favour and just be nice to me and the man in the car and don't get violent and if you've learnt anything from your time in the naughty corner of the trunk of this car it should be that I am sick and tired of being given shitty advice by people that I don't know very well and being made to do horrible things for no apparent good reason—'

'Do you think you could stop shouting,' he says. 'Curtains are twitching.'

I take advantage of his interruption to take a breath, suddenly feeling dizzy, then start again. I can't remember what I said – I was in a highly excited state at this point – but for some reason I must have started waving the gun around, which I only discovered when I clonked myself on the head with it.

I stand panting, trying hard not to cry. When I start talking again my voice wobbles up and down the octaves as if I'm about to hit puberty.

'Sorry,' I say, 'I think I'm a bit tired and emotional.'

He stares at me. I push the gun back into my trousers and squeak as the cold metal catches my foreskin, almost making me pull the trigger. God, I must stop doing that. It's fun the first couple of times but it soon wears a bit thin. Try it if you don't believe me.

'Can I have a hug?' I mutter, forlornly.

He stares a bit harder.

'Okay, well at least be nice to me,' I said. 'And I'm sorry about last night. You pushed me too hard.'

'Not as hard as you pushed me.' He looks at me long and hard. Then huffs out a big old sigh. 'Fair enough,' he says cautiously. 'But I'd like to know who he is. Please.'

'Don't worry about him, he's nobody.'

'How come he gets to sit in the car if he's nobody? And I get shoved in the boot?'

'Look, you can change places now if you want, it's not important—'

'Maybe it's not important to you, you get to drive and decide who sits where. My piles are giving me hell back there.'

'Well, lucky for you I picked up some cream for that back at the….

Look, this doesn't matter just now.' I hold up the lock picks. 'Can you use these?'

'No, I just bought them because I thought they were pretty.' I resist the urge to point out that he has spent the best part of twelve hours locked in the boot of a car and his precious picks haven't helped him get out of that. 'Untie me and I'll show you.' His voice is pretty croaky and I remember guiltily that he hasn't had a drink in about eight hours.

Can I trust him? No. Do I have a choice? No. This will have to be handled very carefully. If I let him get the upper hand then I will have lost my one chance at getting out of this. Plus I certainly don't fancy applying his haemorrhoid cream myself.

And after all, he hasn't given me any trouble since yesterday.

'What about our mutual friend, there?' I ask.

'He's probably better off handcuffed, and I imagine we can't really let him go just at the minute since he probably knows too much, thanks to you and your big mouth.'

I start to argue, but realise he's quite right. As usual.

'Should we off him, then?' I ask, in my best menacing goon voice, which comes out sounding a bit like Sue off *Sooty and Sweep*. I really need some sleep.

Two pairs of eyes stare at me like the loser I am.

'Only joshing,' I say, pathetically.

'C'mon, Mike.' He sighs. Holds out his wrists. 'At this moment we need each other. I'm not about to do anything stupid while you're holding a gun on me.'

Oh yes, the gun. I pull out the gun (carefully) from my trousers and hold it on him whilst I undo the knot at his wrists, watching him closely all the time. Watching his every move.

Paying particular attention as he removes the gun from my hands, nuts me in the face, and then swiftly kicks me in the testicles so hard I swear long-dead distant relatives back in Northumberland must have winced.

I lie down quickly, squeaking like a guinea pig on heat with a mouthful of cotton wool (never heard one? You don't know what you're missing).

Captain America scowls at me.

'You brought that on yourself,' he rasps, then reaches into the front seat and takes out the water bottle. 'I'm in charge now, so let's get a few things straight.'

He takes a huge swig from the bottle, a huge gulp of Backseat Boy's wee, and then spits it out in a rather impressive arc across the street.

God help me, I laugh. I know it's wrong and childish and pathetic but I laugh. I laugh and I laugh and I laugh until he kicks me in the testicles again. And then I laugh no more.

*Tuesday May 4th. Lunchtime-ish.*

So I was running, running, running because, let's face it there's not really much else to do on a Tuesday afternoon when you've just accidentally, um, defrauded…misappropriated funds from…okay, *robbed* a bank *and* you are carrying several thousand pounds of hit money apparently from some Mexican terrorist group *and* you have a particularly vicious-looking handgun tucked into your underpants (have I mentioned how much that chafes when you run?) *and* you know your wife is going to give you such a hard time when you try to explain that either you or she may well end up shooting you, just to make the point that you appreciate, that you understand fully, that what has happened, what you have done, is very, very, very naughty indeed.

After a bit of running (seven minutes tops, maybe a bit less – must start exercising again), I decided that I needed to sit somewhere quiet, turn my lungs the right way out and think things through a little. One of my big problems, according to Anna, is that I spend too much time thinking and talking and not enough doing.

Well. I certainly seemed to be addressing that imbalance at the moment. Or does it not count if you're having things forcibly done to you?

(Actually, the word Anna uses most often isn't *talking* but *ranting*. You're having a rant. You are doing a Rant. I'm being Mr Rant – see how clever my stage name is? These things don't just happen at random, you know.)

I realised I was standing next to the Sensory Awakening Garden for the Visually Impaired that the council put in last year, and it looked quiet and secluded enough to hide a desperate fugitive. In I went.

Nice. I don't know why the place wasn't stacked out. I'm sure your average visually impaired person could get a lot from standing on a pile of broken glass, hoovering up the overwhelming smell of dog shit and the sound of an old alcoholic alternately throwing up and singing snatches of 'I Will Always Love You'. It certainly awakened my senses.

I forced myself to organise my thoughts. A list. A script of sorts, that's the order of the day.

1) I needed to think.

2) I needed to talk to the guy who was supposed to receive the parcel delivered to me and find out where it's from and what it's all about. Preferably without either of us assaulting the other.

3) Before this I needed to go home – avoiding aforementioned wife – and safely hide the gun and ill-gotten gains. Or maybe I should

take the gun with me until I figured out who said recipient of hit money was.

4) In order to do this I would have to avoid the police and/or whoever sent me the money (or rather, accidentally sent me the money – or rather again, sent the money to someone else and had probably since discovered that I was now in possession of it and wished to eliminate all trace of me, the money and the weapon before I contacted the police or ran off to wherever people who steal hit money run off to. The Costa del Sol? Brazil? Bognor?)

I was lost for a moment in the nightmare of sitting in a "Traditional English" Taverna surrounded by wrinkly old villains with no necks and Cockney speech impediments (that's Bognor for you), being hunted by Speedy Gonzales look-alikes, when I realised

5) I needed to find fifty pee for a cup of tea mate.

I shook myself out of the pleasant reverie.

'What?' I said.

'Got fifty pee for a cup of tea, mate?' the Whitney Houston fan bellowed at me, obviously assuming I had some kind of sensory impairment that enabled me to enjoy the hedonistic pleasures around us, not to mention his camaraderie.

I muttered something to do with the Labour party and their promises and stupid bloody theme tunes that even I didn't quite understand, and then an idea came to me all at once.

I didn't have any change on me but reached into the bag and offered the first note I came across. 'Here, take this—' I started to say, but he cut me off with a strangled laugh and bellowed at me again.

'NO – MATE – THAT'S – A – FIFTY – POUND – NOTE – YOU –WANT – TO – BE - MORE – CAREFUL – WHERE'S – YOUR – HELPER—'

'Shut the hell up!' I said, in as friendly a manner as possible under the circumstances. I took off my sunglasses and fixed him with what I hoped was a steely stare. 'Shut up and take the money and—'

'I can't take that!' he bellowed. 'What d'you think I am? Some kind of scrounger?'

I nodded blankly but he didn't even notice in his incensed state. He leant over so that he could get a good clear spit straight into my face.

'I only want some money for a cup of tea, not to set myself up in the bleedin' heroin trade! I don't know what this country's coming to, I really don't, people making assumptions left, right and centre just because you're a bit down on your luck. I fought for this bleedin' country in two Eurovision Song Contests when I used to play trombone, but you just assume I'm a nobody and always have been because of my externals, but you should have a look at me internally, young fella-me-lad!'

I shuddered so hard the gun slipped under my waistband and lodged itself firmly in the crotch of my underpants. I shuddered somewhat harder.

'Ha! That struck a chord, didn't it! You're not so dapper-looking yourself, but do I make assumptions about you? Well, maybe I do but they're not all bad. Coming in here pretending to be blind – I'm sure there's a law against that you know…and…stop fiddling with yourself down there…anyone could come by and I don't want to get picked up for cottaging or summat, leastways not with someone like you and— Why are you crying?'

I wasn't actually crying, it's just the stench coming off the guy was making my eyes water, but I didn't have time to go into it. Another police car had just streaked past the park, siren still going but he was definitely slowing down, looking for something. I eventually managed to pull out the gun, squeaking as I pulled out a fair clump of pubes that had got caught on the barrel.

'Shut. Up.' I said through gritted teeth. Surprisingly, he did. For all of five seconds. We both stared, fascinated, at the twist of curly hair wrapped around the barrel of the gun I was pointing toward him. Then he started up again.

'Oh, I get it. You're one of these bastards that makes old tramps fight each other to the death and then you and your missus shag the winner together. Terrible business that. Read all about it in me chip papers the other day. You ought to be ashamed. Still, I know people can't help their sexuality.'

I really did think I was going to throw up.

'Ah well, let's get on with it,' he said resignedly.

'Just take off your coat,' I said, quietly. 'Please.'

'Can't we go somewhere private?'

'Just do it.'

He did, muttering all the while about the permissive society and privacy issues, then looked around before he asked,

'Is this some kind of reality TV thing? Like, is me mother going to jump out from behind a bush in a minute? Is that Davina woman going to come in and give us a hug?'

I took a deep breath and shrugged myself into his coat. I could feel the hairs in my nose curling. I handed him my jacket and he looked at it disgustedly.

'George at Asda? You've got to be kidding. That's an Armani I gave you.'

I felt grease scrape under my fingernails as I slipped the gun into my new pocket and the carrier bags under the front of the coat. I reached out two fifty-pound notes.

'Get yourself a new one,' I said. 'And a cup of tea.'

'Don't bleedin' patronise me,' he shouted.

I bent down and took a handful of mud from next to the bench and smeared it over my face and hands. Too late I smelt the dog turd and spotted the used condom half buried in it. I sighed.

'You want to be careful, doing that,' he told me, 'there's used needles and all sorts round here.'

I walked away from him, back into the park, back towards home, pulling a greasy old hat from the pocket of the coat as I went. I slipped it onto my head, trying not to think about it as it sat there like a cold cowpat. My scalp started to itch menacingly.

The last of the red-hot Eurovision lovers was still shouting something at me as I stepped back out onto the pavement but I couldn't hear for the traffic, the sirens, the fatty hat pulled down over my ears.

And, believe it or not, gentle reader, this was when things *really* started to turn bad.

I stumbled and twitched the three miles home, recoiling every time a siren went off near me. (Which seemed surprisingly often. How come there are suddenly so many police available when you don't want to see one? You're always reading in the papers about people phoning up and no police appearing when someone's been murdered or mugged or fiddled out of their royalties for a TV appearance, but you rob one little bank and— ranting again, sorry.)

I hunched myself over what was now quite a weighty haul of money and headed for home. It took a couple of hours to weave my way through the back lanes and cycle paths but I got there eventually and as I crept into the street I looked around furtively. No, I don't know what I expected to see – a group of Mexicans in sombreros carrying guitars, stuffed donkeys and Uzis, maybe…

I was a complete wreck, my adrenaline level having at last dipped to a sustainable level, and wanted nothing more than a cup of tea and my bed. And a wash. A long, long wash in very hot water. The thought of hot water and my position in it set me shaking again so I jogged across the road to the house. As I went I reached into my pocket for my—

Bugger.

No, my bugger wasn't in my pocket.

Nor were my house keys.

Or my wallet.

Because this wasn't my pocket and it only contained some greasy cellophane (you don't want to know what was on it – or if you do, then you're out of luck, because I *certainly* didn't want to know what was on it) a battered old equity card in the name of Al Cooper (maybe he was telling the truth about Eurovision – and you don't think it could have been Alice Cooper, do you?) and a booklet from the hospital, cheerily entitled *101 Things You Didn't Know About Impetigo.* My skin began to crawl out from under my shirt and slink off down the street in search of happier times. So that was what my friend in the park had been shouting at me as I left. The fake passport was in the old jacket too.

I sighed. So if the park guy went to the police…

But I was beyond thought for the moment; I really needed a cup of tea. I wandered up to the front door, wondering if I could break in, when I noticed that the door was standing open. My stomach flipped over for the final time and as I deposited the feeble remains of last night's Indian meal onto my own doorstep, I realised that it was Anna's half day. And that I was a dead man.

I thought about just running away and joining a cult. Seriously. Some kind of group for nihilistic failed actors who resent the world and want to bring Armageddon down on the West End as soon as possible. I even started walking back down the path until it occurred to me that there's probably quite a waiting list to join so I decided I might as well face Anna, and the music.

I walked back up the house. It was odd that Anna would leave the door open; something definitely wasn't right. Maybe she was lurking behind the door with a carving knife or a frying pan. Maybe she'd had enough and had left. I have to confess, somewhat guiltily, that the last thought cheered me up for a second, until I realised that however angry she might be – and she was definitely going to be more than a little cross – I needed her by my side right now.

Nevertheless, I was very wary as I entered the hall with a cheery 'Hello! You're not going to believe the day I've had. Now before you start getting upset I have to tell you that none of it was really my fault as…there …was…goodness. You really are in a mood with me, aren't you?'

The house was trashed. There was paper everywhere, furniture overturned, broken glass. I took out the gun from the carrier bag. Not that I would shoot Anna, you understand. I just had the vain hope that maybe I could shoot myself before she got to me.

'Oh Anna! Darling?' I called in as jolly a voice as I could muster. 'Where are you? Promise you won't castrate me before you've heard me out. Come on Anna, you're scaring me. I promise I'll pay you back for the Indian last night and I'll take all of the money to the poliee*eeeeeeeEEEEEK!*'

The back door was shattered. There was blood all over the kitchen, and a note on the table. It seemed to be written in crayon.

WE arE gets wIfeyours
YoU callS aNd gits iNstruCtioNioNs
Calls toNite
ArE shees deads
Miser X

There was a severed finger lying on top of the note, pointing accusingly in my direction.

Reader, I wept.

## SCENE FOUR
## THE BFGIA

*Wednesday 5th. Morning rush hour.*

I am still the designated driver.

I sit on a pair of testicles swollen like grapefruits (my own testicles, incidentally, in case you're wondering) and wince every time I have to press a pedal. As we're now driving through Bristol, this is quite often. The traffic is appalling, as usual, and I can feel a creeping road rage wafting in through the windows and infecting me. I feel like putting my foot down and smashing everything else off the road. I could do it too, as the off-road tank that we've stolen probably wouldn't suffer any more damage than a high-speed train hitting an ASBO kid. It would probably be about as morally questionable, too. I don't mention any of this to my passengers though, as I don't want to give them any more ammunition for hating me. Especially now that one of them has a gun pointed at my head.

We're driving through a rather upmarket area of the city and I begin to relax a little. Hopefully this "friend" of my "friend" is a fairly civilized chap, whatever his murky background.

Then, surprise, surprise, everything begins to change. The shops become seedier, the houses more run down, and every corner seems to harbour a young man in a hoodie, twitching and shuffling and generally being furtive.

Once civilisation has completely disappeared over the murky green horizon, I'm instructed to turn off the main road and up a side street that looks like something out of Oliver Twist. A group of white Rastafarians with a combined hairdo resembling a dried-out cornfield glare at us lazily as we park.

'Go and knock on the door,' says Uncle Sam from the back seat.

I start to protest but he jabs the gun into the back of my head and rasps, 'Just do it.'

I get out of the car.

As I cross to the pavement one of the scarecrows wanders over. He is short and fat and has bare feet. He looks like Frodo Baggins might have looked if the forces of good hadn't prevailed.

'Black, E's, H, acid?' he asks, in a bored Somersetshire voice.

'What?' I ask.

'Coke?' he says, 'Whizz?'

'What do you take me for?' I ask

He looks me up and down.

'How about some nail polish remover?' he asks. 'You can take it home an' have a good sniff, innit like. Loser.'

I lean into his face. 'Take a good look in the car behind me, Drug Lord of the Rings. The fat guy with the pissed-off face and the bandage around his head is an undercover government agent with a very big gun. Now, if you don't disappear in the next five seconds he may well shoot you. If he doesn't, he'll definitely shoot me, and I'm not making any promises that you won't get caught in the crossfire. Now, piss off.'

He stares at me for a second. 'You need some valium,' he says quietly. 'I can do you a good price.'

I have to admit I'm sorely tempted, but there is a sharp clacking noise and we both look around to see Sam tapping the car window with the barrel of the gun and smiling cheerfully. When I look around Worzel Gummidge and his scarefriends are hoofing it up the road.

I walk up to the front door of the flat like John Wayne with nappy rash. I don't know what to expect. Some old guys like Sam, maybe. Some geriatric spy who might be able to help us track down who these madmen are, before they kill us/kill my wife/have us kill someone/kill my chances of ever appearing on *Coronation Street*.

So imagine my surprise when the door opens to reveal a stunningly beautiful blonde Bond-girl type and the biggest, muscliest, most Nazi-esque human being I have ever laid eyes on. He looks like a fridge-freezer with arms. Both of them are holding very large automatic weapons, pointed at me. And neither one of them is smiling.

'Hello,' I squeak.

I think about pretending to be a Jehovah's Witness, but on balance I figure it would only increase my chances of being shot.

'I'm with Sam,' I say. No response. I jerk my head backwards and their guns flick up a couple of inches. Needless to say, this does little to calm me down. 'Sam Smith. Sam's in the car,' I croak. 'He's fine. He just wanted me to—'

'Can you speak up a bit?' says Bond-girl in a lovely refined English accent.

I clear my throat. *Project, man,* I think. Always give your audience your best, even the ones in the cheap seats. And especially the ones with big guns.

'Sam,' I say, as loudly and clearly as I can, 'Sam Smith, he's in the car. He wanted me to check things out and then he's coming in—'

'Stop shouting, for Christ's sake,' says Bond-girl, 'and get inside. And did you just fart?'

I go in and she waves across to the car. Or I think she's waving at the car. Maybe she's just wafting away an unpleasant aroma. But like I said, I can't help it when I get stressed.

As I go in I see Sam opening the car and staggering out, bringing our new best friend with him.

Mr Nazi prods me in the back with his gun and I sashay through to the living room, bow-legged and shaking. The men waiting for us are everything that the gun-toting Nazi is not. Small, shrivelled, short-sighted judging by the great thick glasses they wear, unarmed and in a wheelchair. Or one of them is in a wheelchair, anyway. Maybe he's unlegged, ha ha. The other only looks a very short step away from one. And I imagine short steps are all he can manage at his age. Wheelchair Man looks about a hundred years old and the other chap looks old enough to be his grandfather. The walking dead man grins a toothless smile at me and belches halfheartedly.

'ELL-LO,' says Wheelchair Man, sounding like a cross between Stephen Hawking and Sparky the Magic Piano. 'YOU-MUSST-BE-MAYU-KEL.'

*Tuesday May 4$^{th}$. Afternoon.*

*Admit it, Michael, you're finished,* I thought.

All I could do now was phone the police and hand myself in. Maybe join the Wormwood Scrubs Amateur Operatic Society and learn to sing soprano – bound to be a big hit with the boys.

I was actually reaching for the phone when it occurred to me that if I did call the police, then my chances of ever seeing Anna again would be reduced to nil. Even assuming that whoever had taken her didn't kill her, I couldn't imagine her ever coming to see me. Unless they brought back hanging. Then she'd probably have booked a front seat.

*Think, Mike. What would George Clooney do?*

Hire in a new scriptwriter, I imagined. Or have his name taken off the credits. Or start suing people. That's the American way.

Oh. Hello!

The American. I had forgotten about him. *He* must know what's going on. Hoorah! So, I decided I *would* go to the police if the American couldn't think of a way out of our little predicament – because it *was* ours now. A trouble shared and all that. I felt better already.

I picked up the carrier bags and the gun and a few extra bits and pieces I thought I might need and peeked out through the front door. Apart from the fact that lots of other people were peeking out through their front doors, and disappeared rather quickly when they saw me, everything appeared normal.

I left the front door ajar and walked to the corner with as innocent an air as I could. Pure nonchalance. Gene Kelly couldn't have done it better.

I hesitated at the foot of the path. Looking around in that obviously furtive sort of, *Hey, I'm being furtive, so you pretend you can't see me, and I'll pretend it's working and I can't see you seeing me,* kind of way that all the best amateur spies go in for. Then I see the Big Fat American looking straight at me from his doorstep and it's so obvious that he can see me that I stop being quite so furtive.

'Well if it isn't Mr Stinky,' he said, somewhat smugly. 'Come for another peek at my pants, boy?'

Yes. He did. He really said "boy", just like Rod Steiger in *In the Heat of the Night*. Now I'm no Sidney Poitier, but I did a good impression of righteous indignation.

'And who might you be, boy?' he asked in that sheriffy sort of drawl.

'They call me Mr Rant,' I said, advancing on him until we stood nose to nose in his doorway. Then I thought that sounded a bit silly so I pointed my gun at him. Pointed his gun at him. Well, it was someone's gun, and it was pointed in his general direction, if you discount the wobbling. And he certainly wasn't taking any chances.

He looked a little taken aback, but not quite as much as I would have liked.

'You be careful with that gun, son.'

'Okay, *Dad*.'

'What? What is this, I — Oh. I get it. You're here about some kind of weird paternity shit? Well, let me tell you, boy, taking precautions were as much her responsibility as mine and you ain't gettin' a penny out of me.'

'Just shut up and get inside,' I said, menacingly. Or it would have been menacing if I hadn't sounded like my voice was breaking.

And if I hadn't farted.

'Oh, man, will you stop doing that,' he said, but at least he headed back into the house. I followed, closing the door behind me.

'I'm just nervous,' I said, 'Sorry.'

'Jeeezus,' he said, wafting his hand in front of his nose theatrically. 'Go see a doctor. Do you think maybe you have Irritable Bowel Syndrome? 'Cause it's certainly irritating the hell out of me. Maybe you should try colonic irrigation. Worked for me.'

'If you don't shut up right now, Buffalo Bill, I'll irrigate your colon with a bullet,' I hissed, somewhat testily. *God*, I thought, *I'm something of a natural at this.* Surely I was moving to the dizzy heights of Villain, Second-in-command. I'd have to remember to update my details when I sent my CV in for work next time.

I took the length of washing line out of my pocket.

'Now what in the hell are you going to do with that,' he asked sarcastically.

'Look, it's nothing personal,' I said, 'It's just that I've been having a really bad day so far and I would feel much better if you couldn't jump up and throttle me at any point.'

'I'd feel a helluva lot better if you'd stop waving that damn gun around, but we can't have everything, now can we.'

'Look, just humour me.'

'I am humouring you, boy. I am humouring like you've never been humoured before. You don't want to find out what happens when I stop being humorous because you for one will not be laughing.'

'Okay, look, ha, ha, I'm humoured. Now, let me tie you up and I'll put the gun down. Or don't let me tie you up, and I'll shoot you in the leg.'

'Sounds fair.'

So after a few minutes fumbling and a lot of 'the rabbit goes around the tree and through the hole and then…no, the rabbit comes out through the hole and round the tree and back down the hole' (I never was very good at knots), I eventually got his hands tied together, him tied to the chair, and the chair tied to the table. I debated tying the table to the door but that seemed a bit excessive.

'Okay,' I said, a little breathless from the exertion of pulling on knots and shifting furniture, 'My name is Michael Rant. Call me Mike. Nice to meet you.'

'Likewise,' he said dryly, 'My name is Samuel Smith. You can call me Mr Smith. Or Sir.'

'Okay, *sir*,' I said. 'Now, I have a problem—'

'I wasn't going to remark on that, but as you brought it up, do you make a habit of storming into people's houses and gardens, stinking and waving guns around?'

'No. I'm quite new to this game.'

'You don't say. So what exactly was it that you wanted to talk with me about, young fella?'

'"Talk with me"? "Young fellow"? You Americans don't half talk funny.' The look he gave me threatened to melt the gun, so I hurried on, 'Well, if you'd just let me explain. The thing is, I received a package in the post. It should have been delivered here, but the number fell off our door so the courier got it wrong. And it was a gun and some money. And now they've kidnapped my wife. And I've got lots of money that isn't mine. But not all of it is yours.'

I looked at him. He looked back at me like a dog that's been shown a card trick.

'So here I am,' I said, to clarify matters.

'I think you may have missed out one or two salient points, but you have got my interest,' he said. 'So start again. Slowly. And tell me more about the bit with the package.'

So I did. He seemed to be much more interested this time and just as I was getting to the bit about the bank he stopped me.

'I'm sorry you've been dragged into this,' he said.

'Into what?' I asked. 'What the hell is going on?'

He looked at me, seeming to weigh something up in his mind. Looking back, I imagine he came to the (not unreasonable) conclusion that he could be open and frank with me, as no one in his or her right mind was ever likely to believe a single word I said. Ever.

'Look, it's like this,' he said, somewhat shamefacedly, I thought. 'I work for the American government. For the CIA, to be precise. But don't ever try to confirm it or shop me in because it will all be denied and neither you nor I will ever be heard of again.'

'The CIA?' I sputtered, 'As in the Central Intelligence Agency? My God, how old are you? Are you sure you don't mean the Geriatric Intelligence Agency?'

He didn't even crack a smile.

'I'm seventy-one,' he said, proudly, 'and I'm probably in rather better shape than you. But I'm what is known as a sleeper.'

'I bet – you probably need about twenty hours a day.'

'I'm a sleeper – an undercover agent – and I've been here off and on since the early sixties. We don't work on normal ops, we just collect information and take on duties as required – though there haven't been too many of those recently.'

'What sort of "duties",' I asked, more than a little nervously. 'The sort of "duties" that involve guns and large sums of money turning up on your doorstep early in the morning? The sort of "duties" that involve making people's wives disappear? The sort of "duties" that involve cleaning up innocent bystanders after information has leaked out to them through no fault of their own?'

‘Look, just calm down,’ he said, as I had begun waving the gun around in a way which was alarming to me, let alone him.

‘As I said,’ he continued, still eyeing the gun as I lowered it slightly, ‘one of our jobs is to collect information and set up our own operations in order to help the police here and in our own country. Fairly small scale stuff usually. Now, one of the things we do is put information out onto the net and on the street that there are contract killers available—’

‘Ha!’ I said, somewhat predictably, ‘I knew it, you’re a killer! Now where’s my wife, you bastard?’

I only meant to frighten him. When I shot. I aimed the gun a good six feet above his head and shot into the ceiling. So imagine my surprise when it took a tiny nick out of his left ear.

What a racket he made. He screamed like a goat with asthma on forty a day. Rubbish screaming, really. I’d have been drummed out of acting school for making a noise like that and claiming it was screaming.

‘Oh, calm down,’ I said, halfheartedly, ‘I’m sorry. It’s not like I did it on purpose...’

And so on and so forth. I kept on muttering to myself as I fetched towels and water and bandages and eventually got him cleaned up and us both calmed down.

‘Sorry,’ I said again. And I was. ‘Really. That was unforgivable. I’ll try to behave more like a civilised human being from now on, and if I do shoot you I’ll aim to kill or at least maim you so dreadfully, that you lose consciousness.’

I grinned boyishly but he wasn’t going to be won over that easily. ‘Oh well, have it your own way, you big girl. Now, you were telling me about your contract killing business.’

'It wasn't a contract killing business, Mr Rancid,' he said, sulkily, 'that's what I was trying to tell you.'

'It's Rant,' I told him.

'What the hell are you on about now, boy?'

'My name is Rant. Mr Rant.'

'Okay, we'll do this your way. If you don't want to listen, then you'll just have to figure it out for yourself…coming in here…shot…asshole…missing the basketball…fart…' He slumped in the chair, bottom lip poked out like a soup plate, not looking at me.

'Oh, come on, Mr Grumpy,' I said, placatingly, 'I said I was sorry.'

'Rancid,' he said.

'Grumpy,' I said.

'Stinky,' he said

'Do you want me to shoot you again,' I said.

'You wouldn't dare, Stinky,' he said.

He was right. We both knew it.

'Okay,' I said, 'I'll give you to a count of three and then I'll shoot into the ceiling again and we'll both have to take our chances.'

He thought about this until the count of two and seven eighths and then continued.

'All we do, Mr Rank, is take the names of people who get in touch with us looking to do business and then we pass it on to our offices and they contact the relevant authorities. Then they make arrests or monitor people based on the information we send them.'

'So this happens a lot, then?'

'No, not really.'

'How many replies have you had to the adverts, then?'

'Including this one?'

'Yes.'

'One.'

'Well,' I said. 'How lucky am I? You sit around on your big fat GIA arse for forty years and then on your first successful hit I get sucked in and my life turns to shit in twenty-four hours.'

He looked at my coat. Well, the homeless guy's coat. 'And just how good was your life before?' he asked.

'Don't get smart with me, Big Fat G-man,' I screamed. 'I didn't want any part of this shit!' I retrieved the letter that I'd found in the kitchen and waved it at him, 'Look. They've kidnapped my wife and they're going to kill her if we don't do something.'

'Whaaaa—' he said as he struggled and squirmed and tried to avoid the finger that had been wrapped in the letter as it flew across and landed in his lap. 'What in the name of God…?' he shouted.

'I think it's my wife's finger,' I sobbed. 'Like a ransom demand thing.'

He peered at the finger, looking slightly queasy.

'She has very hairy knuckles, your wife,' he said.

I looked closer. He was right. I hadn't noticed that before.

'And very large hands, for a woman.' He looked at me. 'She's not a transsexual or something, is she? I mean, I don't mind, I just don't want to cause offence…'

But I was too busy laughing. When I calmed down I said, 'It can't be hers. Look at the length of that nail. She's always biting hers, and then she complains about it. God, I was so worried for a second, but now—'

'Can I at least see the letter,' he asked politely.

I put it on the table. He was right. Anna was still kidnapped and somebody's finger had been left behind. That couldn't be all good, now could it?

He looked at the letter spread out in front of him.

'Nice penmanship,' he said, sucking his teeth. 'What's this "we" business anyway? Why should I help you?'

I waved the gun at him again. 'This is your shit, your party. I didn't ask to be invited and you're going to help me sort it out.'

'Or what?' he asked, smiling.

'Or…else.'

There was a long, tense silence. Though I have a sneaky suspicion he was only tense because he was trying not to laugh.

'So what exactly did they send you?' he asked, eventually. 'Before the ransom note thing.'

'Just a gun. Some money.'

'Nothing else? No name, no contact?'

'Just a map of Mexico. I figured out it was probably a Mexican revolutionary thing. Do you think this could be some Mexican revolutionary thing?'

He gave me a look. 'Have you got the map with you?'

I rummaged through my carrier bags and his eyebrows rose as I did so.

'That seems rather a lot of money for one hit,' he commented.

'I, er, yeah. I had an accident.'

'What sort of an accident.'

'I sort of robbed a bank.'

He stared at me again for a moment and then said, '"Sort of." Hmmm. We'll maybe talk about that later. Show me the map.'

I did and he hummed and hawed and squinted at it and eventually said, 'I see.' Which was more than I did.

'What?' I asked, squirming on my seat.

'Look at the reference number for the map. In the top left hand corner.'

I looked.

'010172?'

'That's right,' he said, speaking as though I was some kind of imbecile. Normally I would have taken offence but at that moment in time I found it was still a bit above my head. 'It's a dialling code for a mobile phone,' he explained. 'You get the rest of the number by getting the co-ordinates for the cross they've marked on the map. So it'll be…010172 563893. I think. Either of those 3's could be a 4.'

'So what's it got to do with Yucatan?'

'Nothing, probably. It's just the map they chose to use. It's a system we used to use a lot in the Intelligence Services back in the good old days. Terribly outdated now, of course. Generally only used by rookies and people in a bit of a hurry. Not in general use now as anyone with half a brain could figure it out.' He stopped and looked at me, a little embarrassed. 'Er, you call that number and they give you the instructions as to what they want you to do next. Which is presumably to blow someone out of his or her socks.'

'So I just ring them?'

'Look, perhaps you should go to the police and let them sort it out.'

'I can't,' I wailed, 'they have my wife, remember? If I go to the police they'll probably kill her.'

'Then you'll have to do what they ask.'

'I can't do that.'

'Then the police, and widowerhood for you, it is.'

'But—'

'Look, as things stand you're now the corpse.'

'The what?' I shrieked.

'The corpse. It's old service slang. You're basically the fall guy. The patsy? Look, the situation is this. They have you exactly where they want you and you have to do as they ask, and once you've carried out the mission they can just throw you to the police or special forces or kill you and no one will be any the wiser. Essentially you're the walking dead guy and you may or may not save your wife by doing what they ask but at this point in time you can't really do anything but follow instructions. At least you got cash up front. Corpses don't even usually get that.'

'Thanks for clearing that all up,' I said sulkily, 'I feel so much better than I did ten minutes ago. So what if I find these guys and somehow rescue Anna?'

He looked sceptical.

'Then I can go to the police with the evidence and get this whole mess cleared up?'

'These people are usually very good at covering their tracks. And as things stand the only one who seems to have committed any kind of crime is you.'

He paused while this sank in. The light at the end of the tunnel was beginning to dim. 'And you can try to avoid the police, but I'm not sure you have much chance of that,' he said, looking past my shoulder. 'It looks like you have visitors already.'

I turned and looked out the window, across towards the corner of the street, and saw three or four police cars pulled up outside my house and over the road. This didn't look good. On a scale of not looking good this was somewhere on a par with being caught in the goat enclosure at the local petting zoo with your trousers around your ankles. Not that I've ever done that, you understand. Honest.

'Mike,' he said, in a thoughtful tone of voice which didn't do anything to ease my state of mind, 'what did you do with the envelope that all of this came in?'

'Put it in the bin.'

'In the house?'

'Yes. Or I may have left it on the settee. Anna always tells me off for not putting stuff in the bin straight awa—'

'You *shit!*'

'What? I'm not that bad. I do my share of cleaning and tidying.'

'Look, man. How long do you think it will take the cops – who even as we speak will be wandering into your wrecked, bloodstained, unlocked place of abode and searching it with a fine-toothed comb – how long do you think it will take them to find that envelope, the one with my address on it, and mosey on over here to see why you have packaging addressed to me in your dustbin? Or better yet, on the settee.'

'Hours?' (He shook his head.) 'Minutes?'

'If we're lucky. And please stop farting.'

'Sorry. Look, have you got a car?'

'In the garage.'

'Keys, keys, come on.'

'Michael,' he said quietly. Nobody calls me Michael anymore. Not even my mother.

'What? What, what, what, *what*, WHAT?!'

'It's not good to panic.'

'I never said I wanted to be good, just alive. All right! I won't panic, I promise. But let's go. NOW!'

'Stop. Deep breaths. Now. Do you have anywhere we can go?'

'No. I just want to go away and hide. Please! Help me. I'll give you half the money. Three quarters. All of the money! I'll be your best friend.'

'That's enough to make me want to shout out and fetch the cops myself, right now.'

'Please!'

'Shut up! Keep up that rumpus and they'll be coming over here before they find the address. Now we need to get as far away from here as possible. Is there someone we could stay with that you trust, say in Scotland or—'

'We could go to London. I'd thought about going down there soon anyway. Simon lives down there and he's away for a few months and he said he'd leave the key in a flowerpot in the back garden so I could use the flat whenever I wanted and I wasn't sure 'cause he's been a bit off with me lately after—OW!'

He had kicked me on the shin to shut me up.

'That sounds perfect. Let's get out to the car and—'

'Wait, you are coming with me, aren't you?'

'Well, it would seem that you've rather blown my cover for the moment, so I'm going to need to move on anyway. I'll come with you as far as London and then we can go our separate ways.'

'Oh please don't leave me, oh please, please, please…'

'Look, let's just get moving and we can sort things out when we get there. Maybe I should stick around and see if we can get a lead on these guys.'

'Definitely, definitely!' I was nodding like a toddler who's just been told he can have ice cream if he stops poking the cat with a fork.

'Okay, I'm going to need a few items. Go upstairs to my room, open the walk-in wardrobe and you'll see a computer. Lift up the desk it's on, the whole top, and you'll find two suitcases. Bring them, and then get my car keys from the kitchen. They're on a little hook by the back door.'

I ran out of the room and upstairs. As is usually the case on these estates, I'm basically running through my own house – same layout, same fittings. I looked around as I went up and into the bedroom and couldn't help thinking that I liked what he'd done with the place. Nice use of colour. Not too overpowering. Bit of fancy artwork but nothing that swamped the narrow stairs. And the bathroom! Boy, it was a bathroom to die for. This man obviously had taste. The bath was—

'Rant!' Sam shouted from downstairs. 'What the hell are you doing? We need to get out of here! Now!'

'Sorry, sorry,' I called back, hurrying into the bedroom. The "walk-in wardrobe" was actually the spare bedroom, a poky little room in all these houses, except that he'd walled it in and created a mixed sort of study-cum-storage area. Clever! I'd have to talk to Anna about that.

'Rant! For Christ's sake!'

I hurried to the desk and fiddled with it, trying to get the top to lift off. I couldn't resist peeping around the curtains (nice heavy bit of green twill) and looking across to my house. There were several policemen standing around on the street, one talking to Poodleman, who was looking quite animated. Poodleman that is, not the policeman. The policeman looked rather bored, considering this was probably the most exciting thing to have happened on the estate since it was built. Most of my neighbours were creeping down their drives, desperate to find out what was going on/stick the boot in. It was only a matter of time before one of them said they'd seen me heading in this direction and pointing a gun at a Big Fat Geriatric Intelligence Agent…

*'Rant?!'*

'Just coming!'

I flipped up the top of the desk. There were three suitcases inside, two ordinary sized ones and a small vanity case tucked down the side. I was going to shout down and ask which ones he wanted but I decided it wasn't worth the aggro. I just picked up the lot and staggered downstairs.

Grabbing the keys from the kitchen, I went out through the side door into the garage. I opened up the car (BMW, nice again – being an international man of mystery (semi-retired) must pay well) and hefted the cases onto the back seat, put the keys into the ignition, and cracked open the garage door as quietly as I could. No one seemed to be looking our way.

I crept back to the kitchen and called, 'Okay, Sam. Let's go.'

There was no reply. 'Sam,' I called, a little louder, 'They'll be here any minute. Let's go!'

'Would you like to untie me from the goddamned chair first?' he called back. Quite politely, I thought.

I hurried back in and freed him from the furniture, leaving his hands tied, then helped him out to the garage.

'Hang on a minute,' he said, as I opened the car door for him. He started fiddling with the burglar alarm.

'I think that's the least of your worries,' I hissed. 'Come on!'

'Just…one…sec…there we are. Better safe than sorry.' He smiled at me, and though I couldn't put my finger on it, it was a very worrying smile. The kind of smile a cat gets when it remembers it shat in your slippers this morning, right after you forgot to give it some milk.

I bundled him into the car and started it up. I gently eased out into the road and it took all of my efforts to crawl past the police clustered in the road as slowly as possible. I made sure I was rubbernecking as obviously as anyone else just to keep their suspicions at bay. Two policemen came out through the front door, shaking their heads. Carrying a large brown envelope. Time to put my foot down. I started to accelerate, still looking at the police on my lawn, when Sam shouted, *'Look out!'*

I swerved and narrowly avoided squashing Poodleman, who looked as white as his little dog. Both man and poodle stared at me, first in terror, then in anger, and then, recognising me, with a kind of terrified, angry excitement.

I put my foot down and screeched out of the junction at the end of the road, ready to put as much distance between myself and the forces of law and order as possible.

'It looked like they found the envelope,' I said after a couple of minutes of twisting and turning down back streets and footpaths. 'I'm really sorry to have got you involved in all of this.'

'I thought it was me who got you involved, boy,' he said, and there came that wicked little smile again. 'And don't worry. There won't be much left to find by the time they get a warrant and head over to my house.'

'What do you mean?'

'That burglar alarm. It set the timer on the explosive I have hidden in my desk upstairs. It'll blow in about…one minute. There'll be nothing left to find by the time—'

'In the desk?' I asked, with a tone that made him look over at me with concern.

'Yeah, why?'

'Where in the desk?'

'In the small vanity—'

'Out of the car!' I screeched, screeching to a halt.

'What? Why…'

'A small vanity case!' I screamed, screaming faster than I'd ever screamed before, wrestling with my seat belt and throwing the two large suitcases and my carrier bags out through the door at the same time.

'Asmallvanitycase – like the one *lyingonthefloorinthebackofthecar!?!?!*'

I could only carry one of the cases and my moneybags and still run. Sam, with his hands tied together, wasn't carrying anything. He just wobbled off frantically in his slippers. I had had a vague notion of going back for the other case, but as it was I only got about ten yards when the car blew up, sending me flying and skinning my knees. Quite badly.

## SCENE FIVE
## LONDON CALLING

*Still Wednesday May 5$^{th}$. Still morning.*

For a while they have disappeared into the next room while Sam's ear was patched up properly by the Nazi-looking guy and the bandages changed. Nobody seems too worried about my injuries and I give up showing them to my handcuffed companion when he closes his eyes and begins to snore.

They were obviously discussing the situation at the same time because they are gone for quite a while. I can feel myself dozing off when suddenly I am shaken out of my reverie when Sam makes the introductions.

The man in the wheelchair, wearing a bright yellow Lurex jumpsuit that shows off his figure in quite alarming detail, has no hair of any description. Bald, no eyebrows, no eyelashes, no stubble from shaving. Nothing except the two bunches sprouting like carrot tops from his nostrils. He could probably plait them and give himself a Fu Manchu moustache. Sam introduces him as Joshua Smith.

'No relation,' Sam smiles, when I look at him quizzically.

The older (if that's possible) guy, bent over his walking stick like he's been dropped from a great height and impaled on it, and wearing a tweed jacket with leather elbow patches, a deerstalker (no, really), and zip up tartan slippers, is Michelangelo Van Gogh (honest – or that's what they told me anyway). Mr Van G has hair aplenty. It sprouts from every hole and crevice and is somewhat unkempt. His eyebrows are like those clots of hair you pull out of the plughole every six months. And everything looks like it's been blue rinsed. Most of his teeth are missing, and his gums and lips are bright red, giving the lower half of his face the appearance of a small hairy animal that's been shot and fatally wounded.

'Hello, young man,' he wheezes. Coming from him it is, for once, completely apt. Every man in the world must be younger than him. His voice is distinctly upper-class English.

The other two are, Sam guesses, Agent Smith and Agent Smith.

'That's a CIA thing, right?' I ask. 'The "Smith" thing. Anonymity and all that.'

'No,' Sam says, 'just a coincidence.'

I'm not sure if he's pulling my leg.

'Now then, Joshua,' he says, 'how the hell are you?'

'I-AM-VERY-WELL-YOU-OLD-BUG-GER,' says Joshua.

I look at the voice simulator on the arm of his wheelchair.

'COOL-IS-N'T-IT?' he says. Or the box says for him.

'It's one of the newest toys from back home,' points out Sam helpfully. 'It can simulate any voice based on just a few words recorded and played into it.'

'Then why…?' I ask, and then trail off, embarrassed.

'Why does it sound like a robot?' says Sam, cheerfully. 'Because it is one. I mean, it's Joshua's all-time second favourite television character – remember Twiki, the cute little robot from *Buck Rogers in the 25th Century*? He loved it.'

'BEEDLY-BEEDLY-BEEDLY!' says Joshua helpfully.

'Ah!' I say. 'That's…fascinating. Tell me, Joshua, what was your all-time favourite television character?'

'PAM-EL-A-AND-ER-SON,' says Twiki—er, Joshua. 'FROM-BAY-WATCH. BUT-IT-USED-TO-FREAK-PEOPLE-OUT.'

'I can only imagine,' I say.

'Now then, Mr Rant,' says Van Gogh to the floorboards, in a voice very like that of Rex Harrison in *Doctor Doolittle*, 'it would seem that you have a slight problem and Sam here thinks we might be able to help. Perhaps you'd like to fill us in from your point of view.'

'I think Sam could probably do it better than me.' I say.

'Yes, he's given us a brief account, but we'd like to hear it from the horse's mouth, as it were.'

'Horse's ass, more like,' says Sam

'GENT-LE-MEN-PER-LEASE,' says Joshua.

So I fill them in. Omitting none of the details and adding all of the gripes and setbacks and little injustices I have suffered during the last two days. At the end of it all, they sit back and consider everything I have told them and then give me their worldly-wise opinion. That they should go with Sam's version of events after all, as they couldn't follow what the hell I was talking about.

After he finishes (and he does make it all sound a bit petty and trivial – enough to make me wonder whether they'll bother helping me at all) they again sit back and ponder.

Eventually, Van Gogh says, 'Well, this is all rather exciting for a Wednesday morning, isn't it? And you have to speak with them sometime this morning?'

'Yes,' I say.

'Tickety-boo. Don't mind if we listen in, do you?'

'Not at all, old chap,' I say, somewhat sarcastically, 'that would be spiffing.'

'Don't be an arse, old boy,' he says, 'there's a good chap.'

Suitably chastened, I tell them about the arrangements for calling back.

'HAVE-YOU-SPO-KEN-TO-THEM-BE-FORE?' asks Joshua.

Oh yes. I have spoken to them before. And I know this is, in all probability, likely to be another long, incomprehensible conversation.

*Tuesday May 4th. Evening.*

I was bone-tired by the time we got to London. The van we had stolen was pretty heavy to drive and I'd been battered and exhausted before we even set off. My head was still ringing a bit from the explosion and my knees felt like someone had taken an industrial sander to them.

Sam wasn't looking too chipper either. The flowers had set off his hay fever big time and his eyes and nose were streaming. Served him right really. If he hadn't gone on and on at me about bringing the vanity case bomb thing I wouldn't have made him sit in the back.

After the bomb had gone off in the car (leaving little more than a hole in the road, which I'm sure the police are looking into, ha, ha) we had staggered off up a side street, heading in the opposite direction to most of the general public who wanted to see what the hell was going on, me dragging the one suitcase I had managed to salvage. After about a hundred yards, just as I was thinking of jettisoning the case and hoofing it on my own, Sam said,

'Look, over there!'

'It's an undertaker's,' I said. 'You reckon we should steal a coffin, bury ourselves and wait until the heat dies down?' I admit I wasn't thinking too clearly at his point.

'No, fool,' he rasped. 'Next door.'

A florist. A brief thought about pushing up the daisies came to mind, but Sam hissed, 'The van. He left the van unlocked.'

We staggered over the road and sure enough, the van door was open and the keys in the lock. Hooray! So off we sped again, under the guise of Flora and Fauna's Fine Flowers and Fresh Fish Market. I wonder if the owners really are called Flora and Fauna. And is fish and flowers a normal combination? Perhaps they specialised in water lilies. Or seaweed.

When we got to Simon's flat, I dragged Sam out of the back of the van and got him inside as quickly as possible. I'm not sure what we must have looked like at that point, both fairly banged up and me still wearing the tramp's coat to keep off the worst of the rain as I hunted around the garden for the flowerpot that Simon left his spare door key in. I then raided Simon's cupboards and got us both patched up a little bit, though my first aid skills leave a lot to be desired. We looked like extras from a budget version of *The Mummy* that wouldn't make the final cut.

Having found some fresh clothes and dabbed at the worst of the still-bleeding wounds, I decided I couldn't put off phoning my sponsors any longer. Sam had already hooked up the phone to the answerphone so we could record whatever was said.

I braced myself.

I dialled the number that Sam had written down from the map and waited tensely while it rang. Eventually, after about twenty rings, it was picked up.

'What to do you want?' asked a sinister, rasping voice.

'It's me,' I answered. 'Mike Rant.'

'What to do you want?' asked a sinister, rasping voice.

'I got your message,' I said.

'What to do you want?' asked a sinister, rasping voice.

'Look, I've called you,' I said in my most exasperated, I'm-not-going-to-be-pissed-around-by-you-people-any-more voice, 'like I was told to on the information you sent me. Why don't you tell me what I want? I mean, what's the big deal here? And this better be good!'

There was a long silence.

Eventually he said, somewhat sheepishly, 'Well, I can recommend the vegetarian and the pepperoni. They come with free garlic bread.'

'WHAT?' I bellowed. 'What is this bullshit?'

'Well, how about a four seasons?' he said in a panicky voice. 'You get a free bottle of cola with that. And I can throw in some dips.'

Sam was looking at me quizzically, and I covered the phone to tell him what had been said so far. 'Is it some kind of code?' I whispered.

I held the phone to his ear and he quickly ascertained that we had called the wrong number and this was in fact Sergio's takeaway pizza parlour. Luckily and by sheer coincidence they were only a few miles away, so he apologised for his excitable friend, reassured the pizza guy that we weren't mystery shoppers and ordered our supper while he was on the line.

'Forty minutes. So, that four must be a three, try again.'

I dialled the new number.

Ringing.

Then, 'Hello?'

'Hello?' I said, 'This isn't a pizza delivery parlour, is it?'

'Is this being kind of joke? I am not finding funny. Who is this please?' Definitely a thickly accented voice. European somewhere but beyond that I would have been guessing. And as you should know by now, precision and care are my middle names.

'Who is this?' I asked.

There was a pause. 'I wonder if maybe, arse you calling about the job?'

'I may be.' I said. 'Would it be possible to speak to my wife?'

He sounded positively jolly at that. 'So it is you!'

'Who?' I asked, somewhat coyly.

'It is being okay,' he said, so chummily he could have been talking to a long lost cousin. 'I knows who you are, but you are not knowing who it is I am, and I am thinking this is probably best for the moment and perhaps always. You will simply be doing as you are told if you are knowing what is in best interests of yourself, and also those of your wife and your child.'

'Ask him who they want you to kill,' whispered Sam.

I shushed him with my hand.

'Look, there's been a mistake. I think you have the wrong man. The gun and the money were delivered to me by mistake and—'

'I am already being aware of some misunderstandment. Do not undermisestimating me. We are knowing this are some problems with deliveries in your area.'

'Then why...' A cog slowly turned and clunked into place in my head. 'Wait a minute. You said child. My wife and child. You've definitely got the wrong man. I don't even have a child – who the hell have you got there with you?'

'Is your wife and child. Mrs Rant. This is being the voice of the Mr Rant, is not?'

'Look, let me speak to this woman that you think is my wife. I'm sure we can clear this all up quite quickly if—'

'Waiting please.'

There was a long pause, then lots of shouting and ouching and banging about. The ouching didn't seem to be coming from a woman. *Oh my God, that's my girl, alright,* I thought.

And then Anna came on the phone.

'You effing bastard,' she said, fairly sweetly under the circumstances I thought. 'What the eff have you bloody well gone and done now you moron, you better hope these effers kill you before I get my hands on you, you effwit, and I'll tell you something for nothing – you're going to have to find the money that I'll lose from missing work, you wankpot. They wouldn't even let me phone in sick. Can you call them and say we've had some kind of family emergency, that there's a problem at home? They're bound to believe that, most of them have met you.'

'Anna...darling...dearest...my sweet,' this sentence actually took a lot longer to get out than that but it did eventually make her pause for breath.

'Don't call me your sweet, tosser. What do you want?'

'Well firstly I wanted to know if you're alright.'

'Yes, no thanks to you. And if you—'

'What about the house?'

'You bastard! Is that all you can think about? The house?'

'No, it's not that. Have they hurt you, I mean. There was blood everywhere. What did they do to you?'

'Not a lot. Most of the blood came from them. Stephan tried to gag me and I bit one of his fingers. The whole thing just came off in my mouth, it was disgusting. Oh, and I stabbed Giorgio in the bum with that fancy corkscrew your mother gave us last Christmas. I knew we'd find a use for it somehow.'

'Stephan and Giorgio? Nice to know you're all on first name terms'

'Now don't get jealous. They're not a bad lot really. Stephan wants to be an actor but apart from that he seems okay.'

'They're not a bad lot really? What, as psychopathic killers and kidnappers go?'

'What do you mean?'

'Well, they have kidnapped you, haven't they? Or are you just off on some kind of New Age retreat? Purging yourself by sticking corkscrews up each other's bumholes?'

'It wasn't in his bumhole; it was in the fleshy bit.'

('What is being bumhole please,' I heard a voice ask in the background.)

'Well excuse me, I stand corrected. Oh and did they mention? They want me to off someone for them.'

'Off someone?'

'Kill them. Dead. Shoot them.'

That made her pause briefly. 'No,' she said eventually. 'You're making it up.'

'I assure you I'm not.'

'Don't be so bloody silly. Have you been watching *The Godfather* again? And who the hell would trust you to kill somebody and get it right? You're more likely to kill yourself.'

I took offence at that and was about to argue when I realised that:

(1) As usual, she was absolutely right. Given how many near-death (or near-really sore) experiences I had had in the last twenty-four hours, I could hardly criticise *her* judgement.

And

(2) It was probably better not to panic her, as God only knew what damage she'd do if she thought I was telling the truth.

'Never mind why,' I said instead, trying not to sound too huffy. 'They just are. That's why they're holding you, Anna. To make sure I go through with some stuff they want me to do.'

'I think you've got it muddled up, as usual. Typical of you, you always just see what suits you and lie to the rest of us to cover up how stupid you can be. They said you stole some money of theirs, you gormless effing tosspot, and they want it back.'

'Look, just let me explain— I— Oh, whatever. But listen, they said they had my child. Our child. What child is this? Who the hell have they picked up with you? And could you please make sure they're not in the room with all that bad language.'

I had to hold the phone away from my ear for a few moments and then managed to slip in, 'Whose is the child, Anna?'

'*Our* child, shit-for-brains. I'm pregnant!'

That stopped me. Briefly.

'What! What do you mean? Oh my God. You never even told me.' I was hyperventilating now, about to faint. Sam was looking a bit concerned over by the window, but he quickly shrugged it off and went back to watching out for the pizzas. 'This changes everything. How could you not tell me?'

'What do you mean it changes everything? You mean you wouldn't bother if it was just me being abducted by this bunch of rejects from *Allo, Allo*?'

I couldn't think of an answer for that, so I pretended the reception was bad and hissed down the phone, to more bemused stares from Sam.

'How long have you known?' I eventually said.

'I only knew for certain about a week ago. I wasn't sure how I felt about it.'

'About what? About the baby?'

'No, about telling you. I knew you'd overreact. Or *over-act*.'

'What, you can tell Giorgio and Stephan and their gang of armed kidnappers but you can't tell your own husband?'

'You *are* jealous, aren't you?' she said in that superior, I-knew-you-fancied-me-really sort of way that she has when she's feeling flirty. 'Well to be honest they were a lot calmer than you usually are, so I thought I'd test it out on them first. So, what do you think?'

Reader, to tell the truth I didn't know what to think. To be honest, I was pretty much reaching the point where I was incapable of thought.

I noticed Sam was frowning at me.

'We're having a baby,' I said to Sam.

'Yes, I know,' said Anna, 'I just told you that. I want to know how you feel about it.'

'Is she alright?' Sam asked, impatiently.

'Fine, yeah, okay, I think,' I said to Sam.

'Is that all you can say?' Anna shouted, 'You feel fine about it? You think?'

'No, I was talking to Sam,' I told Anna.

'Who?' said Anna.

'A friend,' I said. Sam laughed. 'He's a, er, agent, who's helping me.'

'You've got some acting work?' asked Anna. 'That's great. What with the baby and everything.'

'What?' I asked.

'Don't tell her I'm an agent, for God's sake!' hissed Sam.

'You said you're with your agent,' said Anna.

'Piss off,' I said to Sam.

'What?' bawled Anna, and began to cry.

'Not you,' I said to Anna. The crying was quickly muffled. I could picture her trying to hide it. 'I love you,' I told her. She went quiet.

'Look,' I said, trying to control the wobble in my voice, 'I'd rather do all of this face to face, so the sooner we can get all of this out of the way and get together the better. I love you.'

'I am love you too,' came back in a thick Eastern European accent, 'and I am agreeing that we should be meeting. I am thinking we should get together on the tomorrow. Calling me tomorrow in the morningtime, so we can arranging this. Then we can be getting to know the details of what you arse doing for us and we can be arranging what to do with you wife and childs. We must be being the quick because your wifes is becoming very distressed and I am being worried this leads to violence.'

*You bet it leads to violence,* I thought. *I wouldn't want to be in your shoes, Mr Kidnapper.*

'Can I speak to her again, please?' I said plaintively.

'No. On the tomorrow, Mr Rant. Ciao!'

'Wait!' I screamed. 'At least give me a clue as to what the hell this is all about.'

Sam was mouthing a question again.

'Whom do you want me to take out?' I asked. 'Give me that much information at least.'

There was a prolonged pause and I was beginning to think he had gone. Then he said, 'Okay. Just so that you can be doing your housework, likes a good boy. Your customer he is Bela Barbu. He is making the very interesting movies in Romania. Now I must gone.' And he was.

'Well?' asked Sam.

'Not really, thanks for asking,' I said.

'What's going on?' he asked.

'We're having a baby,' I said.

'Well that's great, boy, but you're not going to be having anything – not even a wife – if we don't figure out what's going on. Who is the target?'

'Er…Bella Barbie?' I said. 'Or something like that. Some kind of director who makes films about Romania, I think he said.'

'You think,' said Sam. He didn't look terribly happy.

'Well I was a bit shocked by Anna's news. And he had a bit of a thick accent,' I finished, pathetically.

'Right,' he said, obviously working hard to keep calm. 'I assume Simon has internet access?'

'I suppose so,' I said.

'DO YOU KNOW ANYTHING AT ALL, BOY!?' He had finally lost it. His face had gone bright purple and he stood up, looming over me and shaking his bound fists in my face.

Luckily, just at that moment the pizzas arrived and we both calmed down. (See, that's all it was. Just a bit tetchy because we hadn't had any supper.)

I paid with a fifty from my bag and of course the pizza guy had no change. I toyed with the idea of tying him up and beating him but decided my life was complicated enough. Instead I told him he could keep the change if he would run down to the local corner shop on his moped, and get us some beers and a couple of bottles of wine. I made him leave his wallet, just to make sure he came back, and guess what? He had loads of change in there. Cheeky bugger. I took a couple of tenners out and some small change.

Happily wolfing down half a pizza and some stale garlic bread, I switched on Simon's computer and waited for it to boot up. (It was next to his bed, so I pulled the sleeves of my shirt over my hands before I touched the keyboard. Well, you have to think of these things. Or I do anyway.)

While I waited I nosed through his bedside drawer. Oh, come on, don't act all high and mighty, we've all done it. I found lots of condoms. And two dildoes. And some KY jelly. And some rubber Laurel and Hardy face masks. Aren't people funny?

I went through and told Sam we were online. He pilfered the pizza slice with all the best bits on and disappeared.

I waited while he clicked and tutted away in the next room.

Eventually the drinks came. (The pizza guy asked for a tip. I told him my tip was, in future, not to leave his wallet behind after he'd claimed he had no change. He called me a poof and did a wheel spin in front of the house on his moped. Then he fell off, called me a poof again and started pushing his bike up the street. Luckily we both saw the funny side. Or I did anyway, and I didn't care whether he did.) I opened a bottle of wine and relaxed slightly for the first time that day. God, I felt miserable all of a sudden. Suddenly the whole situation began to sink in as my adrenaline level dipped.

Me, a dad?

About the only thing I knew about babies was that they were

terribly expensive and made you settle down and get a proper job. Then they could grow up and sneer at you for being stiff and boring and conformist just long enough for them to get someone pregnant and the whole cycle could begin again.

*I'm too selfish to be a father*, I thought. *I'm too busy screwing up my own life to concentrate on screwing up someone else's.* Though Anna would probably argue with that.

And before any of that I had to rescue them from some kind of lunatic fringe of the mafia.

And before any of that we had to finish off all this booze and pizza. Why can't life be simple?

Half an hour and half a bottle of wine later, Sam was back.

He looked at me oddly as he came back into the room and poured a glassful of wine – surprisingly neatly for a man with his wrists tied together.

'You looked in his bedside drawer, didn't you?' I asked, innocently.

I could see he was about to angrily deny it, but then he snorted his wine out through his nose. When he'd recovered a bit he nodded, embarrassed. 'Weird, huh? Which one would you rather be? I mean, which one would you rather have to look at if you were making love to someone?'

'Neither really,' he said. 'I'd just keep hearing someone say, "This is another fine mess you've gotten me into…"'

We giggled.

'Anyway,' he said, 'back to the business in hand. I think the target is a man named Bela Barbu. A Dagestanian "businessman" who migrated to Romania with aspirations to become a politician and take over certain less-than-legal operations there. He just happens to be flying in to London Heathrow the day after tomorrow.'

'A businessman? Dagestan?'

'A decidedly shady business man. Imports and exports are what he writes on his passport, but he usually deals mainly in pornography. And does very well from it, judging by the net worth of his company. And Dagestan is a small republic, formerly Soviet state, pretty much the centre of the new, Russian criminal mafia.'

'There's a *non*-criminal Russian mafia?'

He conceded the point with a slow wobble of his head.

'Hold on,' I said. 'This is about pornography? You're telling me that the people who have kidnapped my wife are trying to steal dirty books?'

'Well…it's more likely DVDs and internet software but—'

'Don't "well" me! God knows what they could be doing to her! She could be tied up on a bed as we speak, with Stephan and Giorgio, being made to…made to…'

'Wear Laurel and Hardy masks?' suggested Sam.

'It's not funny!' I can feel myself on the verge of tears.

'Whoa! Hold on a minute there, boy. I very much doubt this is about pornography. It has to be something else.'

'Why does it? You said—'

'I said that's where Barbu made his money.'

'And?'

'From what I've been able to dig up, it's all pretty tame stuff. I mean it's hardcore, but nothing out of the ordinary. The sort of stuff you can buy anywhere in Europe pretty much over the counter of your local convenience store.'

'And?'

'He makes this stuff, or the people who supply him make it, in Dagestan, Romania, the Czech Republic, Bulgaria, Slovakia, where it's cheap. You're talking a three or four hundred dollars budget for making one of these. Three hundred pounds sterling, tops.'

'And?'

'Okay, if, say, you wanted to move in on his business—'

'Which I don't, thank you very much. Even I can earn more than that as an actor. Well…on a good day.'

'—then why, and this is the important bit, why would you blow fifty thousand pounds – that's enough to make a hundred films and have enough copies made to take over a large chunk of the market – why would you spend that money on killing him?'

'How do you mean?'

'You don't have to kill him for his porn. You just make your own if you have that kind of capital. We're talking about what is still an awful lot of cash in Eastern Europe.'

'It's a lot to me, come to that.'

'Yeah, well, imagine if your income was less than a hundred pounds a month. There's no equity union in Romania. Actors are cheap. Porno actors even more so. It's a buyer's market.'

'So what does all this mean?' I was getting frustrated now.

'That I don't know.' I sighed with exasperation but he went on, 'I just know that Barbu must have something else, something much more important. I managed to do a little digging around and he's definitely getting into some heavy political lobbying, both here in the UK and at home. This guy has come from nowhere six months ago to suddenly having a shitload of support from a lot of very powerful people. He must have something they want, and want badly. And I think we can safely assume it's not kosher.'

I thought about this for a moment but it didn't help. I was still completely lost.

'Okay, so what do we do now?' I asked. 'Do you think we can go to the police?'

'No,' he said, 'I listened to the tape of your conversation and there still isn't really anything incriminating on there.'

'But Anna—'

'Even Anna thought you were making all of this up. And your conversation makes it sound like you're taking Mr Barbu to dinner. Do you still have the letter they sent?'

My heart lifted, then sank. I shook my head sadly.

'In my car?' he asked. 'The one you blew up? So we're still a bit sadly lacking in evidence that points toward anyone except you.'

I muttered something about accidents and not my fault and how unfair the world was, but neither of us was listening and I lapsed into silence.

He thought for a moment longer, and then something seemed to occur to him.

'Tell me,' he said. 'Would you have left the address for this place anywhere at home? Anything that might give the police some clue as to where we are?'

'Er – in my address book. And on the letters he sent me. And I think it was written on the calendar as I had some scripts to send back to him.'

He sighed, long and loud.

'Well, I am sorry – as I keep telling you, I haven't had much experience at this game. What does that mean, by the way? As if I couldn't guess.'

'Just that we have to get out of here tonight. After making a few… arrangements.'

I wanted to cry. If ever I really needed to just lie down and drum my heels on the floor before going to sleep, it was then.

'What arrangements?' I asked, though I really didn't want to know.

'I think we have to make you disappear. In a way which will stop them looking for you for a little while.'

'How do you mean?' I asked nervously.

Again he sat and thought.

'Well,' he said, 'you're an actor, aren't you?'

'Duh!' I said. He looked up angrily. 'Sorry. Just a bit tired. Yes, I'm an actor. What of it?'

'Well the whole point of theatre is to make people believe what you want them to believe, isn't it?'

'Yes, I suppose.' I couldn't be bothered to figure out where this was going.

'Well, the first rule is to dress the scene, isn't it? Make it look believable. Then the audience will follow their logic, or rather your logic, and go in the direction you want them to. We have to manipulate them.'

'Go on,' I said, though I knew from his tone that I wasn't going to like this.

'Okay,' he said. 'Now, before you start ranting again, I want you to just hear me out...'

## INTERLUDE 2

*Inspector Mallefant is in a good mood.*

*After the results had come back from the pathology lab (not a place Inspector Mallefant ever visited if he could help it) he had become even more determined to bring Rant to justice and find out what kind of perverted racket he was running. He was also being put under a lot of pressure to stop "this bloody maniac" (as his chief had called him), "find the bloody woman alive or dead, and wrap this thing up before the bloody press get a hold of it."*

*Now it looks as though things might be coming together. He sits in the clean, air-conditioned monitoring station of the Motorway Patrol Unit and gazes at the bright and shiny consoles whilst fresh footage is recorded and rewound, zoomed in on and cleaned up to enhance the image. ("Fresh", "cleaned up" – the very words are sweet music to Inspector Mallefant's ears.)*

*The remains of the car used to flee from Rant's or Grant's residence in Newcastle had been attended by the fire brigade on the outskirts of Newcastle. The van stolen from outside of a nearby florist's shop in Newcastle had been found outside of the burned-out flat of Mr Simon Willoughby-Chase, whose car was, in turn, missing. They had traced the car of this Simon Willoughby-Chase and found it abandoned in Bristol. Another car, some kind of off-road vehicle – "Good for getting through mud and shit," a young constable had explained to a shuddering Mallefant – had been stolen a few streets away. This car in turn has now been picked up by the closed circuit cameras over the M4, M5 and M6 motorways, and is being tracked as it approaches a service station a little way to the south of Manchester.*

*Here there are cameras galore. Another car has pulled in behind the one driven by Rant and four more people have got out and walked over to it. A very large, muscular man; a blonde, attractive (if you liked that kind of thing) woman; a tiny man in a wheelchair with a very large holdall; and a bent little man with a walking stick and some kind of backpack.*

*Rant and a fat man (presumably the missing American neighbour whose car Rant had taken), can be seen getting out of the off-road vehicle and someone else, not clearly visible, stays inside.*

*A call comes through asking what Mallefant wants the four patrol cars to do. They have been following the vehicle driven by Rant since Birmingham.*

*'Just hang back,' says Inspector Mallefant. 'Keep oot of sight, as close tae the target as possible. Ah want tae see whit it is they're up tae. There's something fishy going on here.' Inspector Mallefant, needless to say, does not like fish. Dirty smelly creatures that pick up the shit dropped to the bottom of the sea. He shudders again.*

*'Keep in close radio contact,' he continues, 'and get ready tae move in the second Ah give the order.'*

*Then there is more waiting. There are the quietly given commands to remotely move around the cameras, in order to follow every step of the unfolding action. There are the titbits of information supplied by the twelve officers shadowing the movement of the suspects.*

*Then their main suspect approaches the roadside hotel, or motel, or whatever it is they call these things nowadays, and goes into one of the rooms.*

*Inspector Mallefant asks one of the teams to get closer, to see if they can hear anything. He knows that they will only get one chance at this, and then the anti-terrorist shower will step in and take over, what with explosions on the streets and foreign involvement. For the moment, however, he is not too worried, certain as he is that everything is under control, all avenues covered.*

Softly, softly catchee monkey, *he thinks. No unnecessary macho posturing, all sweaty glands and testosterone. He shivers involuntarily, and forces his attention back to the screens in front of him.*

*Then there is more waiting, and some useful information is inadvertently supplied: the suspects are armed, it would seem. As are the people they are meeting.*

*Then, suddenly, it is decision time. Do they move now or wait and see what develops? It is a tough call, but Inspector Mallefant sees himself as a man who can take the burden of responsibility.*

*They wait. In the meantime members of the public are discreetly moved to a safe distance. There are a few arguments from people who value their motorcars more than their health, but on the whole people come away in a quiet and orderly manner.*

*And then they wait a little longer.*

*Inspector Mallefant wonders if he dares pop out to the toilet, as he is getting a little on the desperate side.*

*Just then there comes a 'What the bloody hell…?' from the men on the ground, and things begin to speed up.*

*There is the 'What in the name of God was that, then? Did you see what they…?' from the men controlling the cameras.*

*The 'Jesus H. Christ on a bike,' from Inspector Mallefant's second-in-command.*

*There is the falling silence in the room as everyone stares at the cameras in dumbstruck horror until the images disappear one by one, and the radios of the units on the ground are overcome by static and then fail, one by one by one.*

*And, as he watches the carnage unfold, as events head towards their devastating, unbelievable and now-invisible finale, Inspector Mallefant has the terrible, overwhelming feeling that he has just blown his biggest case, that there will be questions to be answered, that he has no answers for them that will make any sense. That he is in deep doo-doo. And that he has wee'd himself, just a little.*

*Inspector Mallefant is no longer in such a good mood, and he vows that someone will pay. More than that, he vows that he will skelp someone's arse before this is over – and that someone, he sincerely hopes, will be a malicious little piece of vermin called Michael Grant.*

## SCENE SIX
## FIRE IN THE HOLE

*Wednesday May 5th. Afternoon. This day may never end.*

'You know,' says Sam, philosophically, 'I never did know what that song 'Burning Ring of Fire' was about until I got my first bout of piles.'

'Thanks for sharing,' I say.

We drive quietly, enjoying the aesthetic delights of the M2, and it suddenly occurs to me how little I know about Sam. I look across at him and realize he must have been quite a good-looking guy in his time. He looks sort of like a bastard offspring of Robert Redford and Walter Matthau, if you can imagine such a thing.

'So how did you end up in this line of work, then,' I ask.

'What, you're going to go all Californian on me and suddenly act like you give a shit? Vot voss eet een your chiyuldhoood zat mayde yoo intoo thees goverrnment keeelingk macheeeen?'

'Oh c'mon. I'm just making conversation. I don't know anything about you. Your likes, your dislikes, how you got to be where you are today. And what it was in your childhood that made you into this government killing machine.'

'I got to be where I am right now because you stuck a gun in my face, buddy, and I didn't see you worrying as to whether I'd like or dislike that.'

I let it go. After a few minutes he relents. 'I got into it same way as most people, I guess,' he begins. 'Joined the army, did my basic training, scored reasonable on the tests, sat a whole bunch more tests and before I knew it I was signing the Secrecy Bill and then it was off to keep an eye on things in Korea.'

'Wow, you really have been around a while.'

He eyes me sourly. 'One of the prerequisites for joining the Geriatric Intelligence Agency, I guess you'd say.' Then he smiles and continues. 'Yeah, I've seen some things. Korea, Central America, 'Nam. That's Vietnam, in case you don't know.'

'I know, I know. I've seen the movies.'

'I spent about three years in a Cuban prison in the late sixties – undercover, not officially arrested – which was pretty tough, and then I did a lot of to-ing and fro-ing to Khazginjystania.'

'Did you just say the name of a country, or was that a sneeze?'

'Khazginjystania?'

'Bless you.'

'It's an old Russian domain near the border with Mongolia, first kicked back against the USSR in '29 and it's had a history of rebellion ever since. Still going, but they're not so keen on Uncle Sam any more, since we got into bed with the Russkies. And they're much more dangerous than they ever were when I was there, what with the advent of nuclear devices you can hide up your ass, and chemical weapons you can secrete in your nasal passages and infect whole cities just by blowing your nose and leaving it in a trash can.'

'Er – those last two are jokes, right...?'

'Who knows, these days?'

I think about that for a while.

'So how come you're here?' I ask.

'Like I said, things have gotten hairier than old Van G out there these days and spying's a young man's game. I did some undercover work here in the UK and then over in Eastern Europe during the Cold War and just when it was looking like I'd sit out the rest of my days behind a desk in Langley, the chance came to come live over here permanently and keep an eye on things.'

'So why Newcastle?'

'One of my first drops.'

'What do you mean?

'I visited when I was training, I was dropped in the middle of the local derby between Sunderland and Newcastle. Sort of a covert operation to see how I'd cope in a war zone. I only just got out of that one alive. I liked the city though, so I came back when I went undercover.'

'You ever, er...have to...kill anyone?'

He just gives me one of those looks. 'You ever work on a crappy piece of theatre?' he asks.

'I see what you mean,' I say. 'Sometimes you just have to do the work and swallow your morality, and you really don't want to talk about it afterwards.'

'Exactly. I'm not real proud of a lot of the things I've done, but I did what I felt was necessary, or rather what I was told was necessary at the time to maintain the land of the free and the home of the brave and support democracy and the balance of power in the new world order. And saw myself a few flying hogs while I was about it. But you know how it is yourself – doing the necessary thing isn't always the same as doing the right thing.'

'See, that's the problem,' I say, 'most Americans seem to think it's necessary for them to police the world and that we'd all fall apart if it wasn't for you. Don't you think we'd survive if you weren't over here sticking your noses in?'

'You really have no idea, boy. This island would be long gone if it wasn't for the US of A.'

'We'd have managed,' I say, and notice he's grinning again. 'What?'

'Well, it's just I couldn't help but notice how good you were at "managing" yourself over the last couple of days. I didn't come running to *you* for help.'

'And I wouldn't have needed help if it wasn't for you stirring up the Eastern European Mafia and bringing them knocking down my door.'

'Touché.'

'So what is your job right now?'

'Like I said, sitting and watching, intelligence-gathering, occasionally sticking out a wet finger to see where the wind is blowing from. And hopefully, most of the time, it isn't blowing out of some crazy Limey's butt.'

With that image to ponder upon, we lapse into a companionable silence.

‘This is a new one, though,’ he says after a while. ‘This whole connection is new to me. There have to be some bigger players involved somewhere down the line, but I’ll be damned if I can see who they are.’

‘Why do you say that?’

‘The money, is one. And two is the fact that these guys don’t seem to have any criminal connections other than small potatoes. That means someone is covering for them, keeping them under the radar, and they must have a good reason for doing it.’

‘Good ol’ American conspiracy theories at work.’

He smiles. ‘We’ll see,’ he says, in a not-very-reassuring way. I wonder what else he’s keeping from me. Then he says, ‘Keep an eye out, we’re almost there.’

The service station is less than a mile ahead on the M2. I pull off on the exit ramp immediately before it and into a layby, as we’d arranged. I called our contacts earlier this morning, had a protracted and confusing conversation with the main man (hereafter known as Principal Goon, or PG for short), and finally made arrangements to meet them as soon as we could drive up here.

We left Bristol less than three hours after we’d arrived. I was tired. Really tired. As if the last forty-eight hours hadn’t been stressful enough, a night without sleep hadn’t helped to put things into a better perspective.

The others are following in Joshua’s specially adapted car, which looks kind of like a black Popemobile, and we are going to meet with them, briefly, to discuss our plan of action, as the drive up will have *given everyone a chance to find a little inspiration,* as Sam put it.

Luckily there is a roadside snack-van-cum-salmonella-incubator parked up and I get bacon butties and coffee for everyone. Our miserable passenger says he is a vegetarian, so he only takes the coffee and the bun, though I notice he licks the greaseproof paper it came wrapped in quite happily. (Later, when he thinks we are otherwise engaged, I reckon he'll filch the bacon out of the ashtray and eat it. Can't say why – it's just that some vegetarians do give off that sort of sneaky air underneath their superior front, like they'd have your shoes off you and boil them up to make stock if you turned your back.)

A few minutes pass and then Joshua's car joins us. Nobody bothers to get out; we just wind our windows down and chat happily, passing a tartan flask of tea around like a group of old fogies on the Saga trip to hell.

'We'll drive around the car park a few times,' Sam says, 'just to get the lay of the land. When we find out where they are, Mr Rant and I will meet with them and find out what it is exactly that they want us to do and when. Agents Smith and Smith will scout the area and verify whether Mrs Rant is being held anywhere in the hotel or at the services.'

'Yes, sir, Mr Smith, sir!' barks Nazi Agent Smith. American.

'Okey-dokey,' says Bond-Lady Agent Smith. Posh English.

'Joshua,' Sam continues, 'you will give us twenty minutes and then will provide a distraction so that we can vacate the area safely.'

'BEEDLY-BEEDLY,' says Joshua.

'And Van G, you take out any networks and provide cover for the rest of us. All clear? Any thoughts? Questions? Good, let's roll.'

'What exactly does that mean,' I ask Sam, once we are back on the motorway. 'That bit about taking out any networks.'

'We have to assume they will have some sort of radio or telephone contact and backup of their own. Van Gogh will simply throw a bit of a spanner in the works and block or distort any radio, microwave or video links until we have control of the situation. Also, if any police or secret services are around, it'll stop them accidentally eavesdropping on our communications.'

'He can do that?'

'As easily as falling over. And you only have to look at him to realize how easily Mr Van Gogh can fall over.'

'And what's with Agents Smith and Smith?' I ask. 'They don't seem to quite fit into your little…unit.'

'Well observed,' he says drily. 'No – Sebastian, the big lumpy fellow, is Joshua's great-nephew. Joshua called him to get a little backup and he thought it would be kind of cool.'

'Cool?'

'Those boys don't get out much.'

'What about the other one? The woman. And please don't tell me her name is Belle.'

'What?'

'Doesn't matter.'

'Don't know much about her. Abigail, I think her name is. She and Sebastian are stationed at the US air force base near Bristol for "observational" purposes. He dragged her along for the party.'

I drive a little further.

'We're going to have to be very careful here,' Sam says, craning his neck around to look out the back window.

'Why do you say that?' I ask, as it seems such a ridiculously obvious thing to say.

'Well,' he says, 'it's those four police cars that pulled off the motorway behind us, overtook us and then waited until we passed before starting their engines again. I'd lay pretty good odds that they're following us.'

‘I did wonder about that,’ I say.

‘Still,’ he concludes, ‘too late to worry about it now. We’re here.’

As directed we drive around the car park until the police cars get fed up and park, watching us circle like water going down a drain. We park up and wait until the others drive in and park behind us.

They get out and wander over to our car whilst Sebastian helps Joshua out and into his wheelchair. Van Gogh is sporting an enormous rucksack and looks like a hairy turtle. Joshua is carrying a holdall in his lap that hangs over the sides of his motorized wheelchair like a body bag. (I hope it isn’t a body bag. And if it is a body bag, then who’s it for?) He has also put on a balaclava and camouflage makeup that is beginning to run and smear on his sweating face. But it’s nothing that will make him stand out too much from the hundreds of other aged commandos using the services, I’m sure.

‘Cops,’ says Sam, as we all watch the patrol cars drive slowly past and head off for the petrol station.

‘WE-SAW-THEM,’ says Joshua.

‘Try to immobilize them if you can,’ says Sam, ‘or at the very least keep them well away from us until we’ve finished with the contractors.’

‘Well, they certainly won’t be speaking to anyone in a minute,’ Van Gogh says to a pool of motor oil on the tarmac in front of him.

‘Everybody ready? Off we go. Take no prisoners and anybody left behind is to shoot themselves.’ He looks at the expression on my face and adds, ‘Joke.’

There was lots of okay-ing and sir-ing as we got out of the car. Sebastian and Abigail disappeared among the cars whilst Joshua and Van G headed over towards the restaurant and petrol station.

‘I wonder where they’re waiting,’ I ask, looking over towards the restaurant area. (How these people have the nerve to call these glorified greasy spoons "restaurants" beats me. If that's a restaurant then I'm an international mediator. And the prices! I tell you, I once went into one of those places and picked up a bar of chocolate, a can of pop, and a banana and when I got to the till I said to the spotty highwayman working there, 'I'm terribly sorry, I only have a twenty pound note.' He said to me, 'That's okay, just put the banana back and you should have enough.')

'I think that might be them,' says Sam.

I follow his gaze as he nods towards a group of three men in garish non-natural material suits and designer knock-off sunglasses standing at the doorway to a room in the Highway 2 Hotel. They are waving gaily.

'Discrete, aren't they?' says Sam. 'Like I said, we're obviously dealing with professionals here. Do you have the weapons I gave you?'

I nod uncertainly.

'Just remember to hand over the ones I told you to,' he says quietly, 'and keep the others hidden. A show of good faith at the outset and hopefully they won't search us too closely.'

'Do you really think we'll have to use them?'

'Probably not. Especially if Anna isn't here. We can't afford to do anything too rash until we know where they're holding her.'

That made me feel better.

'Once we have that information though,' he continues, 'then it's fire at will and the devil take the hindmost.'

I stop feeling better.

We walk over to where our contacts are waiting, the three of them looking like a catalogue photo for the Sartorial Polyester Man Collection, smiling radiantly and standing sideways on to show off the bulges under their ill-fitting jackets. All heavily armed, as anticipated.

'Mister Rant I am presuming,' says the smiling man in the middle, whom I recognize as Principal Goon from his telephone manner. 'How the devil are you being, this finest after the noon?'

His hair is greased straight back from a very high forehead and his face is pink and scrubbed, which contrasts somewhat jarringly with his matching lime green shirt and tie and buttercup yellow suit. He has a fifties-style pencil moustache – which droops down under his jaw line at the sides of his mouth and gives the impression of a ventriloquist's dummy – and white patent leather shoes with crepe soles, above which half an inch of red sock is showing. He looks like a spiv on acid.

Left-Hand Goon (bottle blonde with ginger highlights) has on an electric blue suit and orange shirt, with a white leather tie. Right-Hand Goon (big black quiff complete with kiss curls in front of his ears) has on a pink jacket and black trousers. The pair of them also wear white footwear, though Right-Hand has on winklepicker cowboy boots. Dear God, my wife is being held to ransom by Showaddywaddy.

'I've been better,' I say quietly.

'Cheering up!' he shouts. 'Soon all of this is being out of our behind and we can be going back to doing our business as is usual. Can you be improving who you are?'

Sam mutters something about how there's certainly plenty of room for improvement in my case and I remove the severed finger from my pocket.

'Ah!' says PG. 'Is good you are pulling out the finger,' he smiles but it quickly vanishes when he gets no response. He takes the finger from me. 'I will be returning it. Stephan has been missing this. Is something to put his ring around. Now, to the business, if please.'

As arranged, we carefully open up our own jackets and hand over our handguns – replicas, which are the feint to hide the fact that we also have pocket cannons shoved in socks, backs of trousers, and in Sam's case, taped to the middle of his back. I told him when I was fixing it that there was no need for tape as he could just tuck it into the folds of fat on the back of his neck but he'd cheerfully slapped me on the forehead and when I stopped feeling dizzy I quietly finished the job. Probably using a bit more sticky tape than was strictly necessary.

RHG and LHG give us a quick frisk, but they are too busy eyeing up a busload of Japanese students that has pulled into the car park to really pay attention to what they're doing. Plus the fact that neither of them seems too keen to get close to my coat. It really is the perfect disguise, in some respects.

'I am having to confess that I am being a disappointment that you are not being here on your only. Why are you bringed this your father, Mr Rant?'

'It's not my father,' I say, 'this is the man you intended to recruit for the job in hand. I brought him in case he could give me any useful tips on how to exterminate unwanted…vermin.'

'And your name is being?'

'Just call me Mr X,' says Sam.

'Mr X-Lax might be better,' I can't resist, but nobody seemed to find it funny. I need to work on my international material, methinks.

'Coming inside,' says PG, 'We are not wanting to be drawing the attention of the publics.'

You could have fooled me. RHG and LHG step to the sides and we follow PG into the motel room.

The blinds are drawn and the room seems awfully dark after the bright sunshine outside. My adrenaline level quickly dissipates when I realize that Anna is not here, and though I peep around the bathroom door, I know it's too much to hope for. When I look back, RHG and LHG have settled onto the twin beds and are reading comics.

'Your Mrs Rant is quite being safe, but as you are able to seeing she is not in this place,' says PG, reading my mind. 'You must be having the patient.'

I am too disappointed to speak, so Sam takes over.

'We'll be needing some proof that she is alive and well,' he says.

'Off course,' says PG and picks up his mobile phone. He dials a number quickly and hands the phone to me.

'Hello?' says Anna's voice.

'Hello, darling,' I say, my voice tired and cracked. 'Are you okay?'

'Who is this?' says Anna.

'It's me, darling.'

'Me who?'

'Me Mike, your husband!'

'Oh God, hello. I didn't recognize you. What's wrong with your voice? You better not have started smoking again or—'

'Listen, Anna, please listen for once, for goodness' sakes. Are you okay?'

There is a long pause.

'Anna?' I say into the silence.

'Am I supposed to be listening now or talking?'

I can't help but smile. She's fine. 'I love you Anna.'

'I love you too. Now you listen. Did you phone work like I asked you to?'

'Oh, er – I…er—'

The phone is taken from my hand during the barrage of abuse that follows and PG smiles at me. 'Is lively wife you are having. She is full of the sperm.'

'I hope you mean *spunk*,' I growl.

RHG and LHG snigger until PG snaps at them in a language I don't understand and they go back to lounging like the lizards they are.

'What you are thinking of our rooms?' asks PG, indicating the cheap plastic furnishings and the garish flock wallpaper that looks as though it was stripped out of a seventies Indian restaurant and painstakingly transplanted here, complete with stale scents of grease and curry.

'Is nice, no? We are not having such nice hotels where I am coming from. These is nice decors, like on *Changing Rooms*, no? Please! Do not be sitting on the bed.'

This last is to me, his nose wrinkling at the thought of sharing his sheets with my filthy attire.

'And so to the business,' says PG, holding out a file with a photograph pinned to the top.

It shows a fairly nondescript, kindly looking middle-aged man in a very nice wig. The photograph must have been taken on a windy day as the aforesaid hairpiece was standing up like a meerkat on a boulder. 'This is your...how is it said...taggart?'

'Target?' I suggest.

'Ah yes, target. Thanking you. He is a kind of a compatriot of mine and very bad man. He is being over here on business venture. Buying some buildings for the conversion into flats or some such rubbish. When he is at meeting you must take him out and his mens also. And you will brings to me the briefcase which he is having with him.'

'How do you know he *will* have it with him?' asks Sam.

'Is too worth much money for him. He keeps with at all hours.'

'And what's in it?' Sam asks, innocently.

There is a long pause.

'I cannots am telling you this or otherwise I am having to kill you.' He smiles at us indulgently. 'But I will doubling payment already given to you for safe delivery of this items.'

'Do we really have to kill them,' I ask, 'couldn't we just…knock them out or something?'

'Is up to you,' says PG. 'But it is not being easy, and I am reassuring they will not being happy at you. They may come look for you and make you wish you had never been bored.'

'Believe me,' I say, 'I already miss being bored, and I'm looking forward to being bored for many happy years to come. Probably at Her Majesty's pleasure.'

He stares at me for a second, obviously wondering what the hell I just said, then says, 'Oh ha, ha, ha, is being good joke, yes? You Englands you are liking the sarky, no? But towards the point. You are better killings, for my sake and your. I am knowing that for one, I am not liking thought of him and his significant others coming upon my backside. But see, our gender is being very loose, and we are needing the bump quickly to making the rest develop.'

Sam and I stare at him as he frowns, and then has a rapid, quiet discussion with his colleagues.

'Excusing,' he says to us, 'Our *agenda* is being very loose, but we are needing the *hit* quickly to making the *perogies*.'

RHG and LHG are giggling again. 'Progress,' whispers RHG. In a flash, PG whips out a cane from under the covers of the bed and whacks RHG twice across the knuckles with it. RHG makes a noise a bit like Scooby Doo when he sees a Scooby Snack disappear down a drain, and the room goes quiet.

He looks closely at Sam and me to make sure we are taking him seriously and lowers the cane to his side, still swishing. As he lowers it he catches himself on the calf. *'Aiiee.'*

Somehow I keep a straight face, but I don't dare look at Sam.

'So,' says PG. 'We must tighten our shit and get to the rooting. Barbu is in England for short time only and must be done now. Details are all in file. You can be doing with it?'

'Well—' I begin.

PG cracks the cane on the bedside table, making everyone jump. It sounds like a gunshot. *Please,* I think, *don't come running in here to rescue us, please.*

'Is yes or no answering,' shouts PG, going even pinker. 'Do not be pulling on my conkers, little shitty England or your Anna will be swimming with the fishes and you are having had the chips. You can be doing with it or no you can be doing with it?'

'I can be doing with it,' I mutter.

I notice a shadow on the blind and try to catch Sam's eye. I try to subtly twitch my head toward the window and wink at him at the same time.

'What is?' says PG, irritated and flicking his cane back and forth between us. 'You are getting the fit?'

'No, no,' I say, 'just a bit stiff after all the driving and running around I've been doing.'

'Maybe you think somethings is being funny, hmmm? Somethings you are wanting to share with rest of class? I am meaning group.'

Suddenly there is a commotion outside. A *twang* and an *oooooh!* and a *nyah, nyah, nyaaaah*. Like Mr Magoo laughing.

RHG, still sucking on his knuckles and wiping his eyes, runs outside, and returns seconds later.

'Is sleeping policeman sleeping outside window there,' he says, very calmly under the circumstances.

'You have bringed police here?' shouts PG, raising his cane. Gunfire begins to crackle outside the window. 'This is being serious error on part of you. Your Mrs will not be the thankful wife for this.'

I pretend to crumple from the waist, weeping, when he says this (let's face it, it isn't hard, I have all the motivation and emotional memory an actor could need right at the moment), then burrow into my sock and pull out the gun that Sam had given me.

'Alright,' I say, 'Enough of this. Just tell me where she is, you bastard.'

The two goons go for their bulges, but Sam is way ahead of them. He casually reaches behind him and, with a loud ripping sound and a wince, he pulls out the very large gun I'd attached there. Everyone freezes.

'Is mistake,' says Principal Goon, in a voice that lets me know he's not bluffing. 'I am issuing warning. Shooting me is death certificate for the lady. Do not be asshole, Mr Rant. Same is going for you, Mr Rant's friend.'

PG is right. It's a stalemate. A Mexican standoff, or whatever they call them in the movies. All we can do now, all *I* can do now, is follow orders and hope that they live up to their end of the bargain.

I begin to back towards the door, pushing Sam along behind me.

'Okay,' I say, 'We'll do as you ask. But I am issuing warning too. If you harm one hair on my wife's head I will hunt you down and I will pull on your conkers so hard that the hairs on your head will disappear and sprout out of your arse. *Capice?*'

PG gulps and nods and when I take a quick peek over my shoulder even Sam looks impressed.

'Bring her to London,' I continue. 'Tomorrow. I will phone you and arrange a time for the swap. Be ready. And remember what I just told you.'

He nods. 'I am think that maybe you are right man for job after all, Mr Rant,' he says, extending his right hand to shake on our agreement. I pointedly ignore it and turn away from him.

There is the constant din of more and more people running and shouting outside. I risk a quick glimpse through the half-open door and I spot Joshua in his wheelchair firing off handfuls of firecrackers with a catapult. They travel quite a way. An armed response unit keeps popping up from behind various parked cars and I see one of them duck as a firecracker bounces off his helmet then skips off the roof of a car and hurtles off towards the petrol station. They seem to be uncertain whether they are allowed to shoot at ancient men in wheelchairs bearing fireworks.

I'm sure they will have no such qualms when it comes to me, so I duck back inside, lift the burnt orange plastic blind and gaze out of the window towards the petrol station.

Which promptly vanishes.

It is replaced by the biggest fireball I have ever seen.

The entire hotel seems to jump up into the air and settle down, somewhat broken and rearranged, with an almighty thump. The glass from the window is gone but luckily most of it is in the blind, which is now an even more burnt orange.

PG and the others throw themselves to the ground, screaming. I'm a bit of a sheep when it comes to situations like this, so I promptly join them.

Sam drags me to my feet, tutting.

We both look out of the gap where the window used to be and suddenly there are police and Japanese tourists everywhere.

Agents Smith and Smith are happily shooting them where they stand.

I understand by the amount of time it takes them to fall over (and the fact that they stand there like Ecstasy ODers at a rave, looking at their hands and smiling), that they are not really shooting them, merely knocking them out with some kind of tranquilizer darts. But I'm not sure if this will make anyone feel particularly better when it comes to explaining things in court.

It's definitely time to leave, and we begin to head for the door.

One of the men (RHG, I think) suddenly jumps to his feet brandishing a gun, which he is pointing at Sam. Out of pure reflex, I jump at him and grab him around the waist and neck – just as Sam shoots him with the taser gun.

My new best friend and I do a very sexy little high-speed samba around the room while Sam tries frantically to turn off the power.

It appears Sam isn't quite used to this particular toy yet as the power being supplied to us energizer bunnies seems to be increasing. My dance partner makes a noise somewhere between the Crazy Frog and a Clanger, then says *pooh!* and faints clean away.

Sam is suddenly leaning over me and shouting, 'Mike? Mike, are you okay? We have to go now, can you walk with me?'

'Nyah,' I say.

'Is that a yes or a no?'

'Nyah,' I say.

He picks me up bodily (he really is stronger than he looks) and half carries, half throws me to the door, keeping the gun trained on the men on the floor.

'Everybody be cool,' he says, 'and stay exactly where you are until we're out of sight. We'll speak to you tomorrow, gentlemen.'

I am dragged back out into the sunlight where all hell has broken loose. There are policemen and women lying on the ground all around us, and Mr Agent Smith is pushing Joshua in his wheelchair towards their car. Under his arm he is carrying a small man with a now familiar style of garish suit and a bag over his head. Ms Agent Smith is leading Van G along by his stick (if you'll pardon the image), practically dragging him off his feet and gesticulating towards us. All the while, Van G is fiddling with the laptop slung around his back. 'Get out of here, now, sirs!' she yells at us.

My whole body still feels numb from the shock treatment administered by Sam. He helps me as I walk spastically back to the car. For a moment I see myself from outside, moving jerkily along like something from an old silent movie, with a soundtrack heavy on the trombone.

'Whiss 'appnin?' I manage to gasp.

'Looks like Joshua got a little carried away with his distraction,' Sam mutters.

'Smgglibassano?' I say.

At that moment two Japanese men leap out in front of us, cameras whirring away like grasshoppers on speed, shouting, 'You smile, you smile, is TV show, yeah? Cool!'

Out of what can only be pure reflex, Sam shoots both of them in less than a second and they stand grinning and muttering 'Ooooh. Arigato,' and then pitch forward onto their faces, cameras still whirring, probably catching the full glory of my melted shoes to be used for identification purposes later in court. Must remember to ditch them.

Sam throws me into the back seat, where my head lands in the lap of our reluctant fellow traveller, slams the door, and then runs round to the driver's side. I slowly pan my head around and notice that Van G and Ms Agent Smith are still a long way away. In fact they can barely have moved more than six feet. Ms Agent Smith is beginning to look somewhat panic stricken and shooting at anything that moves. And a few things that don't.

'Shit on a stick,' shouts Sam, starting the car and swinging it in the direction of the odd couple. He drives straight at them and at the last second screeches into a U-turn around them and jumps out to help Ms Agent Smith get Van G into the back seat on top of me, to the accompaniment of rapturous applause from a group of Japanese schoolgirls.

'I say,' pants Van G, 'Impressive driving, old man. Thought you were coming straight at us. Almost soiled meself for a second there.'

And then we are all in the car and driving very, very fast and I know we are in great danger, but my mind begins to drift back, back, back to happier times...

As we circle around, trying to avoid the policemen who seem to pop up from behind every car and wall, I realize that I am losing my grip on both my consciousness and my bacon butty.

Round and around we go. Round and around and around...

## SCENE SEVEN
## FIRE IN THE HOLE 2: THE PREQUEL

*Tuesday May 4th – Wednesday May 5th.*

We had driven around the building four times.

I was about to go around a fifth time when Sam complained he was getting dizzy and could I just get on with it.

'That's easy for you to say,' I complained, 'you probably do this kind of thing all the time. I'm sure this has got to be *so* illegal.'

'It is illegal,' he said (not at all) reassuringly. 'But standard operating procedure dictates that we use all necessary means to carry out our mission to a successful conclusion – even if it means bending the law.

After all, we do have diplomatic immunity should things go wrong on an operation—'

'No, you have diplomatic immunity,' I reminded him, 'I have an underused Equity card and immunity from nothing. Well, possibly measles and TB. Though they may well strip me of that if I'm caught. And test out the smallpox virus on me while they're at it.'

'Well, let me put it this way,' Sam whispered from the back seat, 'your situation isn't likely to be made any worse by what we're about to do. And it may just buy us the time to work out exactly what's happening and figure a way out.'

I pulled over and parked and we stared out at the grey floodlit building ahead of us.

'Well?' said Sam.

'Well, what?' I answered. Still the master of wit and repartee.

'Untie me, and I'll go and scout out the lay of the land.'

'No way am I untying you,' I said.

'Don't you think I may look a tiny bit suspicious going in like this?'

'That's your problem. Anyway, you're the international spy and master of disguise. You'll think of something.'

'And what makes you think I'll come back?'

It was a good point.

'Okay,' I said, 'let's go through it one more time.'

Five minutes later I was creeping stealthily down a corridor, invisible to all but the closest scrutiny, when a uniformed security guard wandered over and told me that the STD clinic was closed for the day and if I was looking for the homeless shelter it was half a mile down the block, around the corner and follow the smell of the canal. And watch out for the dealers and the gangbangers down there. And maybe I should think about having a shower while I was there. I thanked him and went outside into the drizzle for five minutes while Sam made *'What?'* gestures from inside the car, then hurried back through the corridors, pausing only to get the same detailed information as the security guard had given me from a nurse, a secretary, a doctor and two cleaners.

Eventually I found an unlocked changing room (do these people have no idea of security? No wonder the NHS is bleeding money). I made sure there was no one around and went in to borrow what I needed. Once I had a white coat on over my grubby attire everyone seemed to just ignore me and within five minutes I was back outside pushing a patient trolley.

'Everything okay?' asked Sam as I opened the door.

'So far, so good,' I said. 'Where do we have to go?'

Sam gave me directions from memory – though he did say it had been a while – then he jumped up on the trolley (well, I say, *jumped* – he sort of rolled on, holding his bound wrists out in front of him, puffing and panting and all the while complaining about how cold it was and couldn't I have found one with cushions on) and I covered him with the sheet I'd borrowed.

With Sam on there it didn't seem to run quite as smoothly as it had before. Every few yards I'd find myself bashing into a wall or door and each time Sam would let out a muffled groan, which sort of added to the effect but drew rather a lot of unwanted attention. Needless to say, when I manhandled the trolley around the last corner and bashed through the double doors I was sweating like a pig and swearing like a troop of troopers.

Imagine my surprise, then (though why I should even have been surprised, given the way everything else had gone so far) when I pushed the trolley into the middle of a room and found twelve rather swollen ladies staring back at me from the beds, open-mouthed.

'Hello,' I said. There was no reply so I pressed on, 'Seem to have gotten myself lost. New here, you see? Is this by any chance the morgue?'

Two of the women shrieked, presumably in horror at the thought that they may have passed on without even realising, three clutched at their stomachs, as though to block the ears of the unborn children inside, a couple more peered around and one jumped up and looked under her bed as if to check there were no corpses secreted under there. Then all twelve of them started pressing their call buttons for the nurse.

The nurse came running in, obviously peeved to have her tea break interrupted. I say this not because I think NHS staff are lazy and do nothing but sit around drinking cups of tea all day, but because she had a cup of tea in one hand and a rather full bedpan in the other.

'What's going on here?' she demanded.

'Sorry, er, Staff Nurse Simpson,' I stammered, reading her name badge, 'I seem to have gotten myself a little lost, new here, you see? Doctor, um...Crackenthorpe's the name. How do you do?'

She glared at me balefully. 'What happened to your head,' she asked finally.

I put my hand up to the bandages. 'Oh...I...er...tripped over one of the patients. Dropped down dead right in front of me. Most inconsiderate. Lucky he was dead, let me tell you.' I laughed awkwardly.

'Just lost a patient,' I continued, 'Well, not lost, actually, he's here on me trolley, ha ha, ahem...but he passed away and we have to get him to the morgue, pronto, and see that he's not contagious.'

She took a step backwards and explained where I had to go whilst everyone else in the room held their breath and folded whatever material came to hand over their faces.

'Well, carry on as you were, ladies, keep up the good work,' I called cheerfully as I strained to turn the trolley around. 'My wife's expecting too, don't you know? We're hoping for a—BASTARD!'

This last wasn't strictly true, married as I am – it was because I'd lost my grip on the trolley and sent it crashing into a collection of drip stands and bedpans that were piled up in the corner, which slid over and landed, with much clanging and clattering, on top of Sam. Who let out a long, low groan and started calling me things that I won't write down here in case my mother ever gets hold of it.

The nurse stared at me.

'My God,' I shouted, 'It's a miracle! I'd better hurry and get this chap down to A&E immediately. Excuse me sister—er, Staff Nurse—could you just hold the door for me there…? Thank you very much, bye now, bye—!'

I toddled off down the corridor as fast as I could and a few minutes later we were in the morgue. Sam shuffled off the trolley and glared at me.

'Well done,' he said. 'You certainly made a good job of that, didn't you?'

'Well if you'd sent me to the right place—'

'Oh, shut up, for God's sake. We better do what we need to do as quickly as possible because pretty soon this place is going to be swarming with security.'

I couldn't fault his logic there so I moved off into the huge, cold, white-tiled room, not really wanting to look too closely at any of the tables but knowing there wasn't much choice.

'What about this one?' I asked, flicking at a toe-tag.

Sam peeked under the sheet. 'It's a woman. You're not a woman, are you?'

'Not last time I looked.'

We wandered further into the room.

'Here,' said Sam.

Much against my will, I went over and looked under the sheet he was holding up. A blond man with a grey face and sunken eye sockets looked back up at us. Or rather, didn't.

'He doesn't look much like me,' I said. 'I was hoping for someone a bit better looking, to be honest. And he's flabbier than me…'

'It really isn't going to matter, fool. The important thing is he's about your height and weight and hasn't been identified yet. Let's get him up onto the trolley.'

I rolled the body up in the sheet as Sam stood and watched. Then I slid my hands under the shoulders of the body. I squirmed at the cold feeling.

Sam still stood there.

'Well?' I said.

He jiggled his bound hands in front of my face.

'Kind of difficult tied up like this…' he said.

I considered for a moment. Then pulled out the gun again.

'I'll be watching you,' I said.

'Good,' he smiled. 'You might learn something, fool.'

'Okay, Mr T.'

I untied him. Making sure I gave him a nasty Chinese burn as I did so.

He rubbed his wrists for a second, glaring at me, obviously calculating, then moved down to the foot end of the body.

It was a bit awkward, what with the gun in one hand and both eyes on Sam, but we managed to get him transferred over onto the trolley, trying to be as respectful as possible. Though all the grunting and swearing probably lent the lie to that.

Eventually, sweating and panting, we got there.

'Right,' said Sam. 'Under…the…trolley.'

'What…?' I said 'Why…me?'

'Because…everybody and…their dog…has seen you…and you'll…probably…be arrested…on sight.'

'Oh…' I said, 'kay.'

I took off the white coat, and he slipped into it as I climbed under the trolley and gripped the cross struts.

'I'm pointing the gun at your kneecaps, by the way,' I told him.

He grunted and we set off. He then proceeded to bounce me off every wall and door and windowsill he could find. I'm sure it was deliberate.

He was stopped a few times and given my description and said he thought he'd seen me heading out through the back doors. Good thinking. One or two of the questioners still seemed suspicious and lifted the corner of the sheet, apologising and quickly dropping it when they saw the poor guy underneath.

Then, with one last bone-sickening crunch, we were back out in the car park and there was wet tarmac under me. I clambered out stiffly, my ears ringing.

'Nice driving,' I said.

'Now you know how it feels.'

'*God* you are such a petty individual.'

'Takes one to know one. Look, let's just get this done.'

Again we struggled with the body and managed to get him into a sitting position in the front seat. We stood catching our breath for a minute and then Sam started to laugh.

'What?' I asked. Unfortunately he didn't catch the tone of my voice.

'Looks like I'm travelling with two corpses now,' he sniggered.

'That's not funny.'

'Oh, lighten up. Be a man, son. What's the worst that could happen?'

'You mean before or after they kill my wife and I get arrested for holding up a bank, destruction of property and grave robbing?'

'It's not technically grave robbing—'

'Enough! I've had enough of you and your snidey comments! None of this would be happening if it weren't for you.'

'Or if you weren't greedy enough to try and keep the cash you were sent.'

'Bollocks. I was confused. Anyone would be in that situation. You and your bloody schemes to catch petty crooks. Bloody American bloody interference.'

'Tell me, is goddamned whining Limey self-pity better? You need us – you're all over us like a rash. You don't need us – it's back to the superior tone and the turned up nose. You people should learn some respect.'

'Respect?! That's rich, coming from a Yank. The only thing you people respect is cash and food. And you worship your food, don't you tubby?'

'Back off, understudy.'

'Or what, you'll fall on me? Call up the GIA and have them come empty their colostomy bags on my lawn? You're a joke!'

He started laughing again.

'What?' I shouted. I was just about at the end of my tether. Several people in the car park jumped and looked around.

He lowered his voice.

'You finally seem to be finding a bit of a spine in there somewhere, boy. Sounding like someone who wants to get things done. Maybe I should hightail it out of Dodge and let you sort out this mess on your own. Yeah, that sounds pretty good to me. I'm tired of changing your diapers and listening to your stupid whiney accent.'

'Actually,' I hissed, 'technically I think you'll find I don't have an accent. This is just what the English language sounds like when it's spoken properly.'

'Fuck you, you superior, sanctimonious, little pri—'

I shouldn't have done it. He was an old man who was just as fed up as me, who was off his guard – and he had been trying to help me.

But I lost my temper.

I pushed him. Only a little push, you understand. The kind kids give each other in the playground when they call each other stupid names.

But he fell backwards over the corner of the trolley and bashed his head on the tarmac.

I was still furious, but more than that I was afraid of what he'd do to me when he got all of his faculties back, old man or not, so I quickly half lifted, half rolled him into the trunk of the car. Then retied his hands even tighter than before. And gagged him.

Boy, was he going to be cross when he got out of there.

Muttering to myself, I climbed into the driver's seat and looked at my passenger. It was going to look a bit suspicious driving around London with a mummy on the front seat, so I pulled the sheet away to expose his head, and then combed my fingers through his hair to make him look a bit more decent.

Somewhere inside I knew this was all *really* wrong, but I'd started down this path, thanks to the bloody Yank in the trunk (see how sneakily the Americans invade us? – I even use the word trunk instead of boot), and I knew I had to finish it. I wound down the windows (between the two of us it was getting a bit pungent in there) and set off back to the flat.

Suddenly the rain began lashing down again. What with the distraction of having a corpse in the passenger seat and my fury at Sam and the fact that I was shaking with fear and exhaustion, I misjudged a turn and ended up skidding the car into a lamppost, narrowly avoiding someone waiting to cross. I smashed my chin onto the dashboard and bit down hard on my tongue.

Dizzily rubbing at my bruised jaw and trying to figure out what just happened I heard a sharp rapping sound. I assumed it was Sam in the boot, trying to get out.

'Pith off, you bathtard!' I shouted. 'I hope you're thmashed to bit-th in there. Thith ith all your fault.'

The rapping came again, much louder this time, and I looked around to see a rather angry policeman staring in through the driver's window.

I wound the window down resignedly.

'Thorry Offither,' I said, 'I didn't thee you there.'

'No,' he said, 'Nearly bloody ran me over you did. And it's not Officer, it's Constable. Special Constable Meads. Are you alright?'

'Yeth, I think tho.'

'Have we been drinking, sir?'

'Well, I can't anthwer for you, but I'm thober ath a judge.'

'Get out of the car, thir. I mean sir.'

'Are you taking the pith?'

'Out.'

I clambered out, feeling the blood running down my chin.

The man in front of me was about five foot one, Indian, and

determined to make his mark on me, I think. He did look inordinately cross, but I supposed it was just the adrenaline after his brush with death leaving him shaky and pumped up. *Get used to it,* I thought.

When he got a closer look at me, however, his expression turned to one of concern.

'Goodness,' he said, 'did you just do all of that in the crash? I think I better call an ambulance.'

He was reaching for his walkie-talkie, and I was reaching out to stop him, saying, 'It'th alright, honetht,' when he spotted my companion in the front seat. He did a double take, walked around the car and then reached in through the open window.

'Your friend doesn't appear to be breathing, sir,' he said, panicking, 'and he's extremely cold. He doesn't seem to be well at all.'

'That'th becauthe he'th dead,' I said.

'Oh, come on, the crash wasn't as bad as all that,' he said, trying to open the door. I think it must have gotten bent in the crash, as it wouldn't go. I think my head got bent in the crash too, as I couldn't stop myself from saying whatever came into it.

'Oh, he wath dead long before the crath,' I said. 'Honetht.'

He stared at me. 'Do you seriously expect me to believe you're driving around London with a corpse in your front seat?'

'Acthually, I'm the corpthe. He'th justht a dead guy.'

Special Constable Meads stopped trying to open the car door and span around, obviously unsure whether to run screaming into the night, reach for his walkie-talkie or whip out his extendable baton. Then he saw the gun I was holding and seemed to be unsure whether to shit or go blind.

'Look, sir, everything's alright, sir, there's no need for violence sir, please, sir, you go on your way and I won't say a word to anyone, honest, sir.'

You know, it's a sad sign of the times this, but I'd been called "sir" more in the previous couple of days than I ever had in my life. Why? Because, more often than not, I'd been holding a very big gun. Is that really what we have to do these days? Threaten people with violence to get a little respect and civility? I'm beginning to see why the Empire was so hard to maintain. It must have cost a fortune in munitions.

'I'm tho thorry,' I thaid, I mean, said. 'You theem like a very nithe man but I'm afraid I might have to inconveniethe you for a thort while. You thee things are jutht a tad mixthed up at the thecond and—'

'I'm having real trouble understanding you, mate,' said Special Constable Meads, 'on account of your speech impediment. Could you just slow down a bit?'

'Don't you "mate" me. What happened to "thir"?' He just stared at me. 'And I don't have a thpeech impediment, I jutht bumped mythelf when I crathed the car.' He stared at me some more. 'Look, jutht get in the car and don't touch your walkie-talkie thingy. Oh, and you better give me your handcuffth.'

'My what?'

'Handcuff-tthhhh!'

He wiped little flecks of spittle and blood off his face and handed them over (the cuffs, not the spit and blood), and I duly locked them onto his wrists and hurried him into the back of the car.

'Don't worry,' I told him over my shoulder, 'ath thoon ath thith ith all thorted I'll thet you free.'

'Could you face the other way when you talk?' he asked politely. 'Please?'

I tried to make some light-hearted conversation as I drove back to the house. You know the kind of thing – 'Thpecial Conthtable

Meadth? Ith that like thpecial needth?' and 'Whothe idea wath it to thpell lithp with an eth?' but my new friend wasn't biting. Or he was only biting his lips and staring at the corpse in the front seat.

'Don't worry,' I said, by way of reassurance, 'I thidn't kill him. We've only borrowed him. Ath a kind of, er...diverthion. While I prove my innothenthe. You know the thort of thing, you mutht come acroth it all the time in your line of work – prove that I didn't kill my wife, or rob that bank. Or accthept lot-th of money to murder thome people.'

He didn't look convinced.

'You thee,' I explained, while a voice in my head screamed at me to shut up, 'we're going to leave the body in my friendth flat and burn it, tho that the polithe – that'th you – think thomeone'th murdered me and they'll thtop looking for me tho I can go and get thome evidenthe that'll clear my name. He'th dead already, tho what harm can it do?'

He stared at me.

'I have to conthede,' I said, 'acthually it doethn't thound quite tho good when I thay it out loud.'

And this, I think in my semi-conscious stupor, is where my troubles really began. From here on in there was no turning back for any of us and just when we thought things couldn't possibly get any worse – well, you've seen how that turned out.

I hefted the body out through the car window and upstairs with very little reward for my efforts (though the look on the special constable's face was some consolation). I removed the things we needed for the journey ahead and sprinkled the flat liberally with paraffin, girded my loins and apologised profusely to this Unknown Soldier. I shot the body in the head and made my somewhat ignominious departure.

It was only once we were on the road to Birmingham that I realised

I had successfully confounded the police. I had successfully covered my tracks and for the moment I was a free man, no longer a fugitive, and, as New Labour would have had us believe, *things could only get better.*

Not.

# ACT II
# **HABEAS CORPUS**

# SCENE EIGHT
# LESSONS LEARNED

*Now*

Happy memories. It all seems so long ago now. A different life. When I still thought I had a life, rather than doing life.

I stare at the cell wall. It has not become any more interesting in the last twenty-four hours.

The same hackneyed graffiti under the same standard-issue window. The same thin grey light filtering through the same shabby blinds onto the same damp stains. The same marks where I threw my dinner plate at it yesterday in anger, chipping the façade.

There are days when I can't remember how I got here, how all of this came about.

But, unfortunately, those days are few and far between. Most of the time the memories are crystal clear enough to make me shiver down to my standard-issue socks, even in bright sunshine.

I am so, so sorry that I got into all of this and what it has done to my wife. If I could take it all back… I can now see all of the points where I went wrong, made bad choices. Hindsight is a wonderful thing.

I have been patched up now, and most of me is healing, though I am reliably informed that I will have a great many scars. Not all of them sexy or endearing, but I am slowly healing.

But there are still some things that I find hard to cope with.

The boredom, for one thing.

In some ways it's nice. I have people who will bring me my meals, do my laundry. I have little or no responsibility for anything. I do not have to worry about money. I do not have to make decisions, simply follow the rules and do as I am told. And the people in charge here are obsessed with the rules. They are jobsworths and anally retentive types who cannot cope with any change from the routine. They will make my life hell if I deviate in the slightest.

Another thing that bothers me is the fact that I am constantly monitored, all day every day. Every movement, every gesture, every word, and every breath I take. They are watching me. Whatever happened to trust?

Though I suppose they are "figures of authority". And figures of authority are not people to whom trust comes naturally. Not when it comes to people like me. I'm sure they resent the money that is spent on us, the time, the effort. I'm sure any one of them would be glad to take me outside and put a bullet in my head, hang me from a tree. But that is not the way things are done in a civilized society.

So they watch me and I watch them and they watch me watching them and so on and so forth. They are hoping they can learn something from me and I am trying to learn as much about them as I possibly can. *Playing the game,* I believe it is called.

They are waiting for me to screw up so they can jump in and scream and shout and say *I told you so! He's a wrong'un right enough, call the Guv'nor!*

I try to be good; but part of me knows that this is just a front and that every second sees me waiting, too. I am certainly a different person right now to the man who set out on this journey. I am beginning to think that we are approaching payback time. Justice will be served. And then it will be over. Soon enough, one way or another, this will be over.

I just have to be patient.

*Thursday 6th May. Shortly before dawn.*

I looked at what was left of me in the cracked and dirty bathroom mirror. I looked like an extra from an extremely low budget zombie flick.

I know what you're thinking: a lesser man would have probably given up at this point, called it quits. Unfortunately I had given up a long, long time before and my options were now somewhat limited.

At least nobody without cataracts would recognise me from the photos and identikit pictures on the television and the newspapers. It would never stand up in court. *You mean to say you recognised the suspect from this? What, had your dog been chewing it? Case dismissed!*

If only.

I remembered little of the journey; I'd only really started to come around when we hit the small backcountry lanes of the Forest of Dean. As we pulled into yet another tiny village, someone (Van G, I think) pointed out that Fred West used to live just up the lane there. Now *there*'s a sign to put up to impress visitors. COME ON IN TO OVER-PIDDLINGTON, MOI LOVER. HOME OF FRED WEST. WE WELCOMES CAREFUL D.I.Y.ERS.

We'd turned into a small winding track and stopped outside a small stone-built cottage where I half walked, half crawled through the door and collapsed onto the moth-eaten old sofa which took up half of the living room.

As I had slipped in and out of consciousness, without really knowing where I was, or why, I was aware of various comings and goings around me. The GIA seemed to have been awake for most of the night, plotting and comparing notes, preparing some plan of action. Occasionally I heard muted laughter and arguments, various hissed telephone conversations, and a string of questions that I presumed were aimed at our Romanian prisoner, who hardly seemed capable of piecing together a coherent sentence in English – but I didn't really take much of it in. I no longer cared. Let the professionals deal with it, as long as I got Anna back in one piece. Ms Agent Smith popped in at one point and gave me a couple of injections to ease the pain. One of them seemed to only increase the pain – or at least give it a new dimension.

'Don't be such a baby,' she said, as I rubbed my arm and tried not to cry. I tried to think up a suitable reply but was asleep before I'd managed to open my mouth.

At around five in the morning, I awoke from lurid dreams about corpses exploding and Anna chasing me around the house telling me I had to clean up before the homeless man got here for sex. I sighed and turned on the radio. The news was full of half stories about terrorist action, explosions, and a gentleman called Mr Rant. Or Mr Grant. Or Grunt, or Runt – and one commentator suggested I was some disillusioned individual upset because he didn't get an arts grant and had gone on a rampage. Not really so far from the truth, if only they knew.

I switched it off and wobbled to the bathroom. My legs felt like they were made of putty and I kept wanting to throw up. Even after I'd thrown up.

I washed myself as best I could and contemplated what little I could see of my sad face in the mirror.

*What the hell have I done?* I thought. *And why is my arm hurting so much?* I felt it; there was a raised bump where I'd been injected. I hoped they hadn't given me the smallpox vaccine just to finish me off.

'Mr Rant,' called Van G from outside the bathroom door. 'If we might just have a word...'

I thought of several choice words I could offer him but kept quiet, instead picking up my shirt and following him back into the country-kitchen-cum-parlour that seemed to be their base of operations.

There were a few winces and low whistles as I walked into the room, and at first I thought they were sympathising with my wounds.

'YOU-REA-LLY-OUGHT-TO-LOOK-AF-TER-YOUR-SELF,' said Joshua.

'Getting a bit flabby, old man,' said Van G.

'Get lost,' I said, 'I'm not in that bad shape.'

'Youse are having the love handlings,' said the Romanian.

'Who asked you?' I shouted.

Sam and Special Constable Meads said nothing. Meads just

hunched over a plate of Ryvita like someone was going to run in and steal it away at any moment. Mr and Ms Agent Smith weren't around.

I sat down, draping my shirt over my bare chest. 'Thank you very much to the *Celebrity Fat Club* panel, now if you have something to say… Could we please just bloody get on with it?'

'Don't you have to be a celebrity to be on Celebrity Fat Club?' asked Special Constable Meads.

'Not these days,' said Sam.

'Who asked you, anyway?' I whined in Special Meads' general direction.

'Children, children. We need to figure out a plan of action,' started Van G. 'Here's what we know. Bela Barbu has a meeting this afternoon in the London docklands. His lawyer and four bodyguards will accompany him, and he will be meeting with certain dignitaries, as yet unnamed, from various government and local authority offices.'

'Why?'

'Not important,' replied Sam, 'we just have to make sure they don't get in the way.'

'The building where Mr Barbu is meeting this afternoon,' said Van, 'would appear to be a purchase he made a few months ago. It's an old disused public building in the East End of London.'

'What kind of building?' I asked, as it seemed like they were desperate for me to ask something.

'An old sewerage works, disused now.'

The three of them looked at me meaningfully.

'Am I supposed to see something important in this? So he's bought a sewerage works. What, he's going to hold us all to ransom and threaten to spread poop all over Ye Olde London town if his demands aren't met? To be honest I'm not sure anyone would notice the difference. It would probably bring more tourists in, if the truth were told, give everything that Dickensian ambience that you Americans love so much. And—'

'MR-RANT, YOU-ARE-NOT-SEE-ING-THE-BIG-GER-PIC-TURE,' said Joshua. Even his voice simulator managed to sound exasperated.

'What bigger picture? It's an old abandoned shit factory.'

'Not the sewerage works, old chap,' said Van G. 'What lies beneath it.'

They all looked at me

I looked back at them. I looked at Special Constable Meads. He flinched and went back to eating his Ryvita.

'Sewers?' I said.

They tutted.

'The *land*, Mr Rant,' said Van G. 'The land that the building occupies.'

'Oh,' I said, 'I see.' But I didn't.

'How much do you think land is worth in London, Mr Rant?'

'I've never really thought about it.' They looked at me. 'A lot?' They looked at me some more. 'Lots and lots?'

'YOU'RE-GET-TING-WARM,' said Joshua.

'And can you think of anything in London that might have affected the price of this piece of land,' asked Van G. I must have looked as blank as usual. 'Think sport.'

'The world shit-shovelling championships are coming to London? Don't look at me like that. I don't know. The only thing I know about sport is that if you are in any way good at kicking things or hitting people then you get paid ridiculous amounts of money and then you get all the juicy acting roles come pantomime season. Why don't you just tell me?'

'No major sporting events that might just have been mentioned in the news recently?' said Sam. 'Think hard now, boy.'

'Look! I obviously haven't got a clue what you're getting…at… ohhh. Are we talking about the Olympics, by any chance?'

'Well done, old chap,' said Van G, as though I'd just successfully tied my own shoelaces without crying. 'And where are the Olympics to be centred?'

'The East End of London.'

'And if someone had, say, a prime piece of brown site land in the middle of what is to become the Olympic village, a piece of land which was bought for half of its true value, what do you think they might be doing now?'

'By brown site, do you mean shi—'

'I mean disused industrial land, Mr Rant.'

'I think I'd be setting something of a premium price on that land and then retiring to a beach somewhere. But hang on, surely none of that matters. Can't the government just step in and slap a compulsory purchase order on the site, then buy it for the going rate? Bela Barbu might be a gangster but he's got nothing on the British government when it comes to getting their way.'

'That remains to be seen,' said Sam.

Before I can ask him what he means by that, he continues: 'In the meantime, it would appear that our buddies from overseas are eager to have our property baron killed off and to get hold of whatever… *paperwork* Mr Barbu is carrying with him. My best guess is that they want the deeds to the land so that they can make something of a killing themselves.'

'So this is all just about real estate? They want me to kill someone for an old factory on the London docklands?'

'Not just real estate, Mr Rant,' said Van G, 'it's actually some rather valuable real estate.'

‘How valuable, exactly?’

‘We don’t know exactly, but the rumour mill is chugging along quite nicely, and conservative estimates puts the property – and the value of hotel lets and usage of it for the duration of the games, not to mention selling it on afterwards – somewhere in the region of three hundred million pounds. Others put it as high as half a billion.’

‘Wow.’

‘As you so rightly say, wow; worth killing for, if one were to be so inclined.’

‘The important thing,’ said Sam, ‘is to get our hands on the cases and get out of there as quickly as possible. Then we arrange to meet the other group, get your wife, and hand them over to the police.’

‘We’re going to the police? Thank God. That’s the first sensible thing I’ve—’

‘After, old chap,’ broke in Van G, and I caught the harsh look he gave Sam. Strange. ‘First things first. The *briefcase*, then your wife, and then the police.’

I was missing something here.

I retreated to the bathroom to finish getting dressed, then realised that I’d left my shirt on the back of the sofa and went back into the corridor. From behind the not-quite-closed door I could hear a muted conversation.

Van G: So do you think he knows?

Sam: Not yet, but pretty soon he’s going to start and figure it out for himself.

Joshua: *(Not quite so muted)* YOU-THINK-SO?

Sam: Will you turn that bloody thing down! Thank you. As for Rant, he’d have to be pretty stupid not to, once everything starts to come out.

Van G: I would have to say that he's doing a pretty good impersonation so far.

(*Cheeky bugger,* I thought.)

Sam: Mr Rant is not nearly as stupid as he may appear. At the moment he's disoriented and under a lot of emotional stress. After today – well, that may well no longer be the case.

Joshua: AND-THEN?

Sam: Then we have a problem.

Van G: And dealing with that problem?

Sam: Is my responsibility.

Joshua: BEEDLY-BEEDLY-BEE.

I retreated down the corridor and made a lot of noise with the bathroom door. Everything went quiet as I entered the kitchen and snatched my shirt off the back of the chair and once again headed for the bathroom to finish getting dressed. Even the Romanian looked a bit sheepish.

What were they up to?

It was fairly obvious that there was more to this whole business than was meeting the eye, but I had thought that we were sharing up until now.

I sat down on the toilet to think.

That didn't work so I just sat.

From outside, there was a sound of a large vehicle pulling up and crunching on the dirt drive. Then there was the sound of a door opening, and then the sound of several voices singing a charming version of 'Puff the Magic Dragon'.

Miserable as I was, my interest was piqued. I lifted the curtain and peeked outside.

*Oh my god,* I thought. *Please no. Pretty please, with sprinkles on, I'll be good for the rest of my life and I will never, ever complain when Anna puts her cold feet on me, nor will I put foreign coins in collection boxes when I visit country churches. Just don't let this be happening to me.*

Crunching up the gravel path came Mr Agent Smith. Behind him, on a Sunshine Variety minibus half filled with disabled children, sat a shamefaced Ms Agent Smith.

Our transport to London had arrived.

## SCENE NINE
## ROAD TRIPPING

*Thursday May 6th. 12pm.*

We sang 'We're All Going On a Summer Holiday'.

Again.

I had lost count of how many times this was. Certainly more than we had sung 'Puff the Magic Dragon', but less than we had sung 'Gilly-gilly-ossenphepher-katzenellen-bogen-by-the-see-ee-ee-ee-ea'.

The three carers were understandably furious with us, and concerned about their charges.

'They don't like change,' said Sophie, 'they just feel more secure in their normal routine. They can get very distressed if something happens to disrupt that.' I looked at the children. I knew how they felt.

'They are quite safe though,' I said. 'Nobody is going to put them in harm's way.' She harrumphed like she didn't believe a word I just said. I wished *I* could believe a word I just said.

I'd chosen to sit next to Sophie on the coach. I didn't much feel like sitting with my gang. They were sneaking around behind my back, talking about me and making plans to do things without me. I they weren't careful I would tell on them. Sophie was in her late forties and had that kind of "I'm gentle and I'll look after you but if you mess with the people I care about I'll tear your head off and pee down the hole in your neck" thing going on.

Arnold, a wheelchair user, spent a great deal of the journey comparing makes and models with Joshua. All of the kids (and the driver and even the other two carers) were instantly enamoured with Joshua and his voice box and decided it was quite the coolest thing they'd ever seen or heard.

Our Romanian friend was chatting away happily to a girl called Evie who did not speak at all on the back seat. I can't imagine she spoke a word of Romanian but she clapped her hands and laughed at everything he said and he looked happier than he had since we kidnapped him, drugged him and tied him up.

Van G looked more than a little disgruntled at the two smaller children, Eric and Gordon, who kept pulling at the hairs that sprouted from his various orifices.

Sam sat alone and silent on the seat behind me, occasionally tapping something into his laptop.

Mr Agent Smith was fiddling with something in a suitcase in the footwell next to the rear doors, and Ms Agent Smith was at the front, talking the driver through where we needed to go once we arrived in London.

Beth – a young girl with Downs' Syndrome – sat on the opposite side of the aisle from me. She kept looking across and smiling at me. I smiled back.

'You look sad,' she told me.

'I feel sad,' I said.

'Why?' she asked.

'Well, my wife has been taken away by some bad men, and I'm trying to find her before they hurt her.'

She thought for a moment. 'A bit like *Die Hard*?'

'Yes,' I said. 'A bit like *Die Hard*.'

'And you're Bruce Willis?'

'More like Bruce Forsyth,' said Sophie.

I found it hard to argue.

'Fuck! Shit! ARSE! Fuck! Shit!' came a voice from the back of the bus. *Right,* I thought, *that's it.* I stood up and rounded on the others.

'Okay, who was that?' I shouted. 'I don't know where you lot think you are but kindly show a little respect and stop swearing in front of these children. You're not at home now.'

Everyone just stared at me.

'Erm…' said Sophie, 'I think you'll find that was Davie. He has Tourette's Syndrome. He does it when he's put into stressful situations. I did try to warn you.'

'Oh,' I mumbled. 'Well. Carry on, everyone.' And I sat back down.

To Sophie I said, 'I used to do street theatre with a man who had Tourette's. He was a knife juggler. Problem was he wasn't all that good so he used to get nervous before his act. Then he'd stand there in the street, throwing knives and axes about and dropping them and saying, "fuck, shit, bollocks" and occasionally just making weird noises.'

'That must have been a sight to see.'

'It certainly drew in the crowds. Look, I'm really sorry about all of this. It was a stupid idea.'

'Actually,' she said, 'It's quite a clever idea. Nobody is going to stop us, are they? I just wish it had been someone else's minibus you stole. Was that true about your wife?'

'Yes, but please don't be nice to me or I'll start screaming and crying and shooting my gun into the air.'

'Like Keanu Reeves in *Point Break*?' said Beth.

I smiled and nodded.

'Beth is a bit of an action film buff,' said Sophie. 'In case you hadn't noticed.'

'What's your favourite?' I asked. Thirteen minutes later Beth ran out of favourites and was moving onto her second favourites when we went over a bump in the road and—

'Fuck! Shit ARSE! Shit! Fuck!' came from the back of the bus.

I smiled indulgently at Sophie, who stood up and glared into the back of the bus. 'Right, who was that?' she shouted. 'I don't know where you lot think you are but kindly show a little respect and stop swearing in front of these children. You're not at home now.'

I looked around and Mr Agent Sebastian Smith (I'm tempted to call him Mr ASS for short, but that would be churlish) looked up and said, 'Sorry, ma'am, but I have a slight problem here. Agent Smith, could you come here a moment please?'

Ms Agent Smith stood and went to the back of the bus. As I watched she tensed and looked around frantically. She whispered something to Mr Agent Smith and then came back along the bus to me.

'Mr Rant,' she said, carefully and quietly. 'I need you to go and assist Agent Smith in the back of the bus. Now.'

'What's going on?' I asked.

'Don't ask questions, sir, just—'

'Oh, I see. You're going to start ordering me about now are you? Well, Ms Agent Smith, you can tell Mr Agent Smith to kiss my bottom if he needs help, because I am fed up to the back teeth with you lot and your—'

'Mr Rant!' she hissed. Then she started whispering very, very quickly indeed. 'Agent Smith is currently engaged in assembling an explosive device with which to distract the enemy when we are on site in approximately,' she checked her watch, 'thirty-seven minutes. The last bump we went over armed the device and the only thing currently keeping your kissable bottom attached to your pig-headed body is Agent Smith's finger jammed into the firing mechanism. *I* am going to go and relieve the driver right now because the minibus will have to be kept completely straight and bump-free without slowing down or speeding up, otherwise the secondary motion detectors will kick in and trip the bomb. That leaves *you* as the only one fit enough and thin enough to fit into the gap so in the absence of anyone better I am asking you *will you please go to the back of the bus and assist Agent Smith?*'

'Why didn't you just say?' I asked huffily, getting up and heading towards Agent Smith. Mr Agent Smith. Our Romanian friend was still jabbering away happily, but everyone else was watching me.

'Just like Keanu Reeves in *Speed*,' said Beth, wistfully.

'More like Vic Reeves on speed,' muttered Ms Agent Smith. I was beginning to resent all of these unflattering comparisons.

At least she thought my bottom was kissable.

I squatted down next to Mr Agent Smith. He looked a bit hot and sweaty. The suitcase he was next to was very large and very full of things that looked like you wouldn't want to be too near them if they went off. I fought the urge to jump out of the nearest window.

'How's things?' I asked, unsure how else to start.

'Not so good, sir.'

'How can I help?'

'I need to dismantle the motion sensor bit of the bomb.'

'Tell me what to do and I'll do it.'

'That's the problem. I don't actually know, sir.'

I looked at him like you'd look at the man in the television casting offices who tells you that you haven't got the part but he doesn't know why as that is not part of his remit but if you leave your details he'll happily get someone to contact the relevant parties and get back to you, hopefully in the next six months.

Mr Agent Smith looked very frightened indeed.

'It's not my fault. A lot of these parts come ready assembled when we buy them. We just stick them together and hope for the best.'

'Hope for the—' I struggled to control myself and my bladder. Deep breaths, Mike. 'What are we going to do?'

'Well, if you'll just look in my rucksack there, sir, you'll find the instruction manuals for the various components. You want the one that says *Simple User Operating Instructions for Motion Detector Component for use in IEDs*.'

'What's an IED?'

'Improvised Explosive Device, sir.'

'Sort of *Bombs for Dummies*, then?'

'Sort of.'

I rummaged in the bag. It took a little while as there were about twenty books and pamphlets in there. Eventually I found the one I was looking forward and quickly opened it.

'It's in Chinese,' I said.

'Near the back,' he told me. 'The English bit is near the back.'

He was looking really quite pasty now. That firing pin must be really pinching.

I started reading. Five minutes later I was at the bottom of the first page.

'What does it say?' he asked me.

'Made in Slovakia,' I told him.

'Anything. Else. Sir?'

'Not that I understood.'

'See if you can find the diagram, we need to figure out which wires to cut.'

I did and we were neither of us any the wiser. The diagram was like a map of the London Underground that someone had scribbled on with crayons.

'Can't we just open up the back doors and throw it out?' I asked.

'My finger is trapped in the firing mechanism, sir.'

'Can't we just open up the back doors and throw you out?'

'Again, sir, the motion detectors would kick in and it would explode either on the bus or in the road behind the bus.'

I peeked out the back window. The motorway was chock full of traffic. I would be lying if I said I wasn't still tempted, though.

'Sir, we are running out of time here. We're going to hit the London traffic soon and Agent Smith will have to use the brakes. What happens then is anybody's guess.'

I looked at the diagram again. It hadn't gotten any clearer in the last few minutes. I couldn't even see which bits related to the case in front of me.

'Where's the motion sensor?' I asked.

He pointed to a flat black box.

'Can I open it?'

He handed me a small screwdriver and I set to work taking the lid off.

'Careful,' he said.

'Careful is my middle name,' I told him, and then dropped the lid into what looked a pile of plastic explosives. There was a moment when neither of us could remember how to breath. And then something started ticking.

I looked up at Mr Agent Smith. The ticking was his teeth.

'Oops,' I said. 'Butterfingers.'

Inside the box was a mass of wires and at the centre what looked like a glass phial full of silver liquid. I pointed at it and looked questioningly at Mr Agent Smith.

'Mercury,' he told me. 'If it moves too far up the tube on either side it will trip the switches and the whole thing will blow.'

'I thought your finger was in the firing mechanism,' I said.

'This is the primary firing system, sir. There's another one underneath, sir, you'll just have to trust me on this, sir.'

That last "sir" was definitely a little on the tetchy side.

Suddenly the bus began to tilt to the left.

'I'm going to have to turn onto the M25,' shouted Ms Agent Smith. 'We're going to run out of clear road here. Hang on back there!'

I watched in horror as the mercury began to creep up the side of the tube.

'Quick,' said Mr Agent Smith, 'Gently lift your edge.'

I did so and the mercury began to slop the other way. I lowered it. Raised it, lowered it. That ticking had started up again.

Ms Agent Smith made it on and off the exit ramp without slowing down. From all around us came the sound of honking and screeching tyres. I gently tilted my fingers back and forth and sweated, gibbering all the way.

After what seemed like an eternity but was probably in reality about thirty seconds, the bus straightened and the mercury settled. But that ticking was really annoying. I looked up at Mr Agent Smith.

'Can you please control your—?'

But it wasn't him. This time it was definitely coming from the suitcase.

'Oh, dear,' I said.

'Indeed, sir. The bomb seems to have detected some movement but not enough to immediately detonate it. The computer inside it will be checking the components one after the other and when it gets to the primary firing pin and finds it jammed it will probably explode. Sir.'

'Probably?'

'I've never made one of these before, sir.'

'How long do we have?'

'Probably less than a minute now.'

'What can I do? Can I pee on it or something?' I was sure I'd seen something like this in a film and I could certainly do with losing some pee.

'You need to cut some wires.'

'Which ones? I don't have a clue what goes to what!'

'We don't have a choice, it's going to explode anyway.'

I picked up a pair of wire-cutters from the floor and bent over to the box. Blue or red? Blue or red? Or orange? Or yellow? Or any of the other hundreds of colours that seemed to be there.

I closed my eyes and put the cutters around the first wire I came across. I was just about to squeeze when a hand gently took them from me, and as I opened my eyes it reached into the suitcase and snipped a yellow wire, a black one and a sort of taupe one that looked like the colour Anna had fancied when we redecorated the bathroom. We went for apricot in the end, which looked more or less the same but was a bit warmer. Allegedly.

The ticking stopped.

I looked up, open mouthed. Then looked down to see whether I had peed myself.

'Beth? How did you…?' I croaked.

'Saw it on telly. On *24*. They had to defuse a nuclear bomb and it had a motion detector.' She peered into the box. 'Just like that, it was.'

## INTERLUDE 3

*Inspector Mallefant is not a happy man.*

*After the events at the service station he has been dressed down by every officer with a rank equal to or above his own. The junior officers and patrolmen are clearly sniggering behind his back and even the cleaning woman had a go. He has been told that he will be made to take responsibility for everything that has happened. It will be him, not the constabulary, who will be vilified in the press. There is a shit-storm brewing, and Mallefant will be at the centre of it.*

*He has been removed from the case and instructed that, as from tomorrow, he will be back on the beat. He has been given a quota of dealers, curb-crawlers and prostitutes to arrest before the end of the week. He has been told he will be working as crowd control at music festivals and football matches for the rest of his career. Dirty work.*

*The Rant case has now been assigned to the anti-terrorist squad and they have spent most of the night debriefing him. An apt description, since he feels as though he has had his briefs removed and been given a full cavity search.*

*His career is over. He knows that all of these measures are designed to force him out before his pension is due in five years' time. And he knows that it will work.*

*As he enters his office, he notices that a package has arrived for him – the footage he has requested from the various stages of Rant's progress around the country.*

*He knows he should hand it over, that it is no longer any of his concern. Not his job. But, partly out of spite against those who are replacing him and partly from a morbid fascination to learn more about this man who has destroyed his life, he opens the package and begins to watch the videos it contains. Nothing jumps out on the first run through, but he immediately begins to watch again.*

*Something is not right. It's tugging at his unconscious, like a pervert in the undergrowth tugging at his trousers.*

*Look everyone! Here is Rant at the bank. See him frown at his gun. See him try to leave the money on the counter. See him get confused. See him try to argue. See him run away.*

*Here is Rant at the hospital. See him shout and wave his arms about, arguing with the fat man. See his disgust as he carries the corpse. See the funny faces he pulls. Here is Rant crashing his car into a lamppost. Oh, do be careful, silly Rant!*

*Here is Rant arguing with the young Special Police Constable, trying to persuade him to leave. Look, he is talking to the boot of his car, silly Rant. Here is Rant ushering the Special Constable into the back of his car at gunpoint. See how defeated and despondent he looks.*

*Here is Rant dragging a corpse into his friend's house, on his own. What hard work he is making of it. The pathologist will insist on showing poor Inspector Mallefant its autopsy Y-incision as evidence that this was not a recent killing. How green Inspector Mallefant went.*

*Here is Rant dancing in the street with his shoes on fire. Dance, Rant, dance! Groovy Rant. See how unprofessional he looks. See him argue with himself, and with the boot of his car again!*

*Look, here is a blurry film of Rant at a service station, bewildered and bemused whilst the world falls down around his ears. He argues with the nasty gangster types. He argues with the large muscled man. He argues with the senior citizens. He argues with the fat man. He is just one big argument.*

*Where is Rant?*

*Here is Rant.*

No, *thinks Inspector Mallefant. This is not Rant. This is not a man acting of his own volition. This is a man who is following orders. Following them badly, and becoming more and more deeply mired in a shit-pot not of his making. The fat man is somehow involved, if not directly in charge. The strange group at the service station is also involved, somehow. And the people in the other car, who were they? Whose side were they on? What has he missed?*

*Someone was merrily leading them up the wrong path.*

*Inspector Mallefant wonders if he should pass this information on. To the anti-terrorism unit. He knows what they are like, their reputation. They are an equal opportunity unit – they will happily shoot anyone who gets in their way, regardless of race, sex, religion or rank.*

*These were men whom Mallefant is happy to see heading off in the wrong direction. He would like to see them with egg on their faces (not literally, you understand). He has to figure out who the other players in this drama are (ho, ho, Rant would appreciate that). The gangster types, the fat man, the muscle-bound hero and the beautiful woman (if you like that kind of thing). But where to start?*

*Then he pauses. Something is afoot. He rewinds the tape and watches the events at the service station again, more slowly, concentrating on fuzzy video of the beautiful woman. He rubs his eyes. Watches again. It can't be. But…*

*Inspector Mallefant glares at his telephone, which has begun to ring. More reprimands, or more sneering from his colleagues? He sighs and picks up the receiver.*

*Into his ear comes a familiar voice. The last person Inspector Mallefant would have expected to call. As the voice explains, things become clear. He stares again at the frozen screen in front of him.*

*And Inspector Mallefant's day begins to look decidedly better.*

*Then the caller gives him the details of what is about to take place.*

*And Inspector Mallefant's day begins to look decidedly worse.*

## SCENE TEN
## MAD DOG AND ENGLISHMAN

*Thursday May 6th. 2pm.*

We arrived at the sewage works a little later than we'd hoped.

In the wasteland that must have once been a courtyard there were an awful lot of Mercedes and BMWs and stretch limos parked up; many of them with chauffeurs, who sat and watched in amusement as Ms Agent Smith backed in and out of a narrow space to park up the minibus.

She and Mr Agent Smith agreed to stay behind with the children and Joshua. They would follow us when they could for their part of the plan. I told Mr Agent Smith cheerfully to pull his finger out.

I stepped from the bus and breathed in the fresh air. Then I coughed a little and covered my nose.

'Still whiffs a bit, doesn't it?' I said to Sam.

I was dressed in an expensive but worn suit that Mr Van G had lent to me. It was rather small on me; the jacket wouldn't fasten and it pulled in tight under the arms, and the legs were about six inches too short and showed off my paisley socks. And it had some rather nasty stains down the front.

My shirt was that peculiar grey that shirts go when they've been left to boil for too long too often. And the brogues I'd borrowed from Mr Agent Smith fitted on my feet like a pair of clown shoes.

In short, I looked like I had just stepped from the back benches of the House of Lords.

Which was the cunning plan.

'Now you know what we're doing, don't you?' asked Sam. 'I don't want you wandering off the script.'

I sniffed the air (which I immediately regretted) and told him in my most lofty manner, 'I'm a professional, Mr Smith. Just bally well trust me, old bean. You see? Got the role down pat already, don'tcha know.'

The look he gave me did not give the impression that he trusted me to find a nut in a squirrel's nest, but we pressed on.

The meeting should have started by then so we hurried in, following a battered red carpet laid out to protect the shoes of the visitors.

As we reached a large room, more like a hall, I went to pass through the door just as another man was exiting. He was a smallish, portly man dressed in a beautiful Italian suit and loafers. He looked a little like Arthur Lowe playing the part of a gigolo.

We almost collided and he said, in a plummy Oxbridge accent, 'Terribly sorry, after you.'

'Ah, thank you, me good man,' I said. 'Nice to find a bit of civility in this day and age.'

'I think civility is a much underused quality,' the man said.

'Sorry old boy, did I say civility. Meant to say servility!' I hooted at my own humour.

And then I looked at his face.

It was undoubtedly Bela Barbu.

I paused, staring at him.

'Is there a problem?' he asked.

'Not at all, old bean, just admiring your…hair. Very nice it is. Where'd you get that 'do?'

He touched his toupee self-consciously, still regarding me closely.

'Do I know you?' he asked.

'Crackenthorpe's the name. Lord Crackenthorpe. But you can call me Crackers – everybody else does,' I hee-hawed like a donkey. 'Glad to make your acquaintance. And this here's me butler, Smithers. Goes everywhere with me. And you are?'

He looked taken aback that I did not know who he was.

'I am Bela Barbu,' he said suspiciously.

'Course you are, old thing, terrible memory for faces. Was just saying the same thing to the wife only this morning. Funny thing was, turned out I was talking to the bally housekeeper!' I hee-hawed again. 'Well, best get down to business.'

'Of course,' he said, 'please take a seat.'

We wandered through into the room, and I could sense Barbu's eyes on me every step of the way.

'Try to tone it down a little,' said Sam. 'We're here to get the lie of the land, not blow our cover before we get through the door.'

'Chin up old man,' I bellowed at him, drawing the attention of the whole room. 'Soon have this dashed nonsense out of the way. Then we can get back to the shootin'.'

We settled down, Sam looking daggers at me all the while, and I glanced around the room. None of the faces were obviously familiar, though I had an inkling I'd seen some of them on the telly and should know who they were. *Must start watching the news more often,* I thought.

Then I did see someone I knew. Something to do with the Olympic committee. An ex-athlete? A fight promoter? He was—Yes! He was a sports commentator on one of the cable channels. Got into trouble for some call-girl thing. Not that I ever watched any of that rubbish. I only knew him because he'd gone on *Big Brother* and got booted off in the first eviction. I think Anna showed me his picture in *Heat* magazine.

See, I do know some important current affairs stuff.

Then a sound system started up, belching out 'If I Were A Rich Man' as Barbu re-entered the room and walked to a small raised dais at the front of the room. Four very large men in matching black suits and sunglasses strode in behind him and lined up behind the stage, trying to look threatening. They succeeded rather well, I thought.

I started tapping my foot in time to the music. I almost got the lead once in *Fiddler on the Roof* in an off-West End production. Then at the last second the director had changed her mind and gone for an all-black production. It got mixed reviews. I think I was better off out of it.

When he reached the platform, Barbu stood behind a lectern and held up his hands like a presidential candidate at a photo opportunity.

The crowd gave some muted, sickly applause whilst the music faded.

'Gentlemen,' he started. I thought that was a bit sexist, but then I had a quick look around and he was right. This particular meeting was a boys-only affair. 'You all know who I am. And I certainly know all of you…intimately.'

He chuckled softly, but nobody else joined in. *Tough crowd,* I thought. With the instinctive empathy of someone who has died on stage many times, I guffawed loudly, clapped and said, 'Oh, jolly good. Well said.'

Everyone stared. Including Barbu.

He cleared his throat and carried on. 'But we are not here to talk of the past, gentlemen. We are here to talk about the future. The future of London. The future of the United Kingdom as a whole. And the future of my own country, Dagestan, and my adopted country, Romania. In my country we are very fond of the English. We are grateful to the help and support you have given us in the past, and now both Dagestan and Romania need your help again.'

'Just say the word, old thing,' I called, 'we'll be there.'

Heads turned to me again. Some of the looks were most definitely hostile this time. Especially the one Sam gave to me.

'You are too kind,' said Barbu, stiffly. 'But, to continue. My country needs strong leadership, as does your own. And with your help, I shall be the man to provide that leadership. But bringing a country out of the past does not come cheap. And that is why we are gathered here today. With your support, I can gather together the finances I need to begin to pull my country into the twenty-first century. I intend to raise my finances right here. I intend to raise it from the blackened earth on which you now sit. I intend to own the London 2012 Olympics. And you are going to ensure that I am allowed to do so.'

There were angry mutterings and black looks from many members of the crowd, but Barbu silenced them with a wave of his hands.

'I see that some of you still need convincing.'

He clicked his fingers and two of the henchmen went out through a small door at the back of the room and returned a few seconds later with two large black suitcases.

I looked meaningfully at Sam. He ignored me.

'So I have a little gift for you,' continued Barbu. 'Each of you will receive a...promotional disk about my campaign to share with your family and colleagues. I am sure that, once having viewed these short – and some not so short – films, you will be in full agreement that what is on the table will be a worthwhile investment.'

All of the audience seemed a teensy bit tense by now. Some were openly sweating.

'So if you could all form an orderly queue, there is a gift for each of you. Come along now. Don't be shy.'

I could bear it no longer.

'Not so fast, Mr Barbu,' I said.

'Ah, Lord Crackenthorpe,' said Barbu. 'You have a question?'

'Er, not as such,' I improvised, feeling Sam tugging violently on my sleeve. 'It is more of a...demand. Old thing.'

'And what might that be – Crackers?'

A few people giggled at this, but I silenced them with a glance.

'That you hand those cases over to me. With immediate effect. If you know what's good for you.'

A few members of the audience looked a bit panicky as I spoke. One or two even rose to their feet and told me to sit down and stop interfering. What a cowardly bunch.

Barbu waved them into silence.

‘And by what authority,’ he asked, ‘do you make such a request?’

‘By the authority vested in me by the Permanent Undersecretary of the Olympic Leisure, Vice and Fairness Committee, who I am here to represent.’ I could almost hear cogs turning in brains all over the room, trying to figure out if the person I had named actually existed.

‘And if you do not immediately hand over said luggage, I will give the command for the armed policemen positioned all around this building to move in and open fire.’

At that point the four very large men who were standing behind Barbu pulled out four exceedingly small guns. *Ha!* I thought, *I knew they were compensating for something with all of that weight training.*

I also wondered if I had painted myself into something of a corner. Sam just sat with his head in his hands, which was no help to anyone at all really.

Barbu smiled at me, unperturbed.

‘I think that you might just be an impostor, Lord Crackenthorpe.’

‘Well, I could just as easily make the same assumption about you, young fella-me-lad. A Johnny Foreigner coming over here and trying to steal our Olympic Games? Who do you think invented the bally games in the first place?’

All four guns were now trained on me.

I gulped. Waited for the shot.

‘Cool!’ said a voice from behind us. ‘It’s just like *Reservoir Dogs*.’

I looked around and there stood Beth.

Next to her stood Davie, looking somewhat agitated. My heart sank.

‘And who are you?’ shouted Barbu, sounding more than a bit peeved at this latest interruption.

‘Fucking bastards!’ Davie shouts, staring straight at Barbu, who pales a little.

Now, I know I shouldn't have done it. It's not big and it's not clever, and it's certainly not PC, but I was improvising on the spot here with a very narrow margin of error in the script. I know that the marginalisation and stereotyping of those with mental health issues is wrong and to be challenged every step of the way and that the language we use is very important. But I did it anyway, for which I apologise unreservedly.

'This,' I said, 'is "Mad Dog" Davie McGraw.'

Davie growled, right on cue.

'He may look like a harmless teenage boy,' I said, moving myself between the guns and Davie, just in case, 'but he is fact a highly trained killer. He is part of a new breed of soldier, and we are creating them as a primary line of defence against terrorist action during the Olympic Games. And he is *ferocious*.'

'Shit on a stick!' shouted Davie.

'Calm now, Davie,' I said, and I meant it. I didn't want anyone to get hurt. Least of all me. 'Now, Mr Barbu. You may wish to rethink your position vis-à-vis your little suitcases there. Otherwise I shall let Davie slip his leash.'

'Motherfucker!' Davie bellowed.

The four gunmen were looking at each other uneasily, but Barbie was not so easily led.

'Lord Crackenthorpe,' he said quietly, 'I think it would best if you leave right now. I will have one of my men escort you to your—'

'Oh, there you are!' came a voice from the back of the room.

I glanced around as Sophie the carer came into the room and took Beth and Davie's hands.

'Sorry,' she said, 'we were just looking for a loo and these two wandered off.'

Barbu was definitely getting a bit cheesed off by now.

'This is a private meeting,' he shouted. 'We can't have all and sundry just wandering in! Who the hell are you and what are doing here?'

I tensed, waiting for an answer that I knew was going to land me in deep doo-doo.

But we were saved by the bell. Or should I say the *Bill*.

A strange apparition entered the room. He wore a plastic see-through mac over an immaculate overcoat. He seemed to have galoshes over his shoes but it was difficult to tell as he had plastic bags over the galoshes, pulled halfway up his legs and tied around his knees with string. He also wore rubber washing-up gloves and a shower cap. He looked more miserable than anyone had a right to look and still be alive.

'Ah would appreciate,' he said, 'if everyone could jus' stay exactly where thu are. And remain calm, if ye wud be so kind.' At least I think that was what he said. It was hard to tell through the plastic mouth mask he was wearing.

'Who the hell is this,' whispered Sam. I shrugged. I had been wondering the same thing. Obviously, so too was Barbu.

'Who the hell are you?' he asked. See, I told you.

'Mah name's Mallefant. Inspector Mallefant.'

We were none of us any the wiser.

'And Ah'm here tae make an arrest.'

'What did he say?' asked Barbu of one of his henchmen.

The henchman shrugged. 'I am not sure,' he muttered, 'something about being an anorexic.'

Barbu frowned some more.

I decided to help out.

'Good show!' I shouted, 'Let's arrest them all. And about bally time too. That's the chappie you want, up there.'

'Shut up, Crackenthorpe,' hissed Barbu. 'What do you want with me? I've done nothing wrong.'

'Nae, sir,' said Mallefant, 'it's no' you Ah've come fer. It's this wee gentleman here. An' hes name's no' Crackenthorpe. Hes names Michael Rant and he's wanted fer suspected murder, robbery and assault. An' those yon shady buggers wi im are wented fir questionin' an all. So if youse will excuse us.'

My heart sank. It was all over.

Then, 'I don't think so,' said Barbu. 'I think we need to have a quiet word with all of you before you go anywhere. My men here will escort you into the back office here and—'

'If you insist on impeding an officer of the law in the kerrying oot a hes duty, sir, Ah may well have to arrest *you* an all. Ah should warn ye that this building is surroonded by armed polismen, and they will open fire if Ah'm nut allowed to walk oot a hyer under mah own poower.'

'I've already tried that line,' I said forlornly. 'Didn't work.'

'Enough,' said Barbu. 'Take them away.'

The four large men in black began to move menacingly towards us, whilst everyone else backed away in unison, forming a ring around us.

'What now?' I whispered to Sam out of the corner of my mouth.

'You tell me,' he answered, not even bothering to lower his voice. 'You've managed so beautifully up to now.'

Suddenly a barrage of cracks and pops rang out. To the uninitiated it may sound like gunfire, but I realised it must be Mr Agent Smith creating his diversion. His big bomb was (thankfully) out of commission but he had improvised skilfully. I saw him dash along a walkway, throwing what I presumed to be tear gas grenades as he went.

The whole room began to fill with smoke. I saw Sophie disappear into the corridor with Davie and Beth, closely followed by Mallefant and then everyone else in the room, with Mr Van G shuffling along in the rear.

Barbu's men opened fire even as he shouted at them not to, and I saw Mr Agent Smith fall and lie still at the head of a spiral staircase. Sam grabbed my arm and started dragging me away from the exit.

'We've got to get those cases,' he whispered, 'it's our only chance.'

We staggered on through the smoke, waving our hands in front of us, eyes streaming, when I tripped over something. I felt along its length, pulling away when I grabbed a handful of testicles. I peered through painful eyelids and saw that it was one of the men in black. He was unconscious but still held his gun. I pulled it out of his hand and a sudden thought made me look to see what he had tripped over.

It was one of the suitcases.

Bingo!

I picked it up and started staggering in the direction I had last seen Sam. I hissed his name a couple of times but there was no reply.

I decided I'd better hurry and started to make my way toward the exit.

And ran full tilt into someone.

I heard him groan and fall with a thump, as I staggered and managed to hold myself up against the wall. I turned toward him, holding out the gun, ready to shoot. Providing the safety catch was off. And I hadn't gone stone blind by then.

'Goddammit, clumsy fucking Limey bastard!'

Sam.

'I know that's you, Rant. Take my hand.'

I reached out and pulled him to his feet. 'I found one of the cases, but I can't see so well. Go see if you can find the other one.'

'I already have,' I said, holding it up. But he couldn't see it. 'Let's go.'

There was movement behind us, the sound of someone searching. I led Sam away from the noise and found an old wooden door, which opened quietly. We sneaked through. The light was dim in here but I spotted a rack of torches and picked up one for each of us, shoving his into his coat pocket and flicking mine on.

I could just make out a spiral staircase going down. I led Sam towards it and we descended. About halfway there was a water pipe, and we paused a moment to rinse out our eyes.

There was also a smell. It got stronger the further down we went.

'I think we're headed into the sewers.'

'Shit!' he exclaimed, holding his nose.

'That about covers it,' I said. 'Maybe we should go back up.'

Then we heard a door bang high above us, followed by the sound of running feet.

We carried on down.

At the bottom the staircase opened into a large, vaulted tunnel, with no clue as to where to go.

'What do we do?' I squeaked. Along the pipe a couple of rats squeaked back. Maybe they fancied me as a potential mate.

'Split up,' he said, 'you go that way, and I'll go this. If you make it, head for the safe house and we'll decide what to do from there. Good luck.'

'How do I find my way out?'

The footsteps were loud on the stairs now. He gave me a few tips and then splashed off into the dark.

Our pursuers were almost on top of me now. For a second I contemplated just giving myself up, but then I thought of Anna.

'I'm coming, babe,' I said, to nobody but the rats. The rats squeaked back, obviously excited and cheering me on. 'I'm coming.'

## SCENE ELEVEN
## THE PIPE

*Now*

The prison cafeteria is noisy, bustling. The clamouring voices seem as though they are being piped in from outside. A scene-setting hubbub. A disjointed chorus of ever-present violence and malevolence.

I keep myself nearsighted. I do not allow my eyes or my mind to focus on anything. I have decided that introversion will serve me well whilst I am here. No joking, no wisecracks from me. I know that I will not survive long in this place if I cannot keep myself closed off. Quiet.

I take the tray that is offered to me and find a seat with the minimum of fuss. Prison slop. Glue and sawdust poured over a chop made from the insole of someone's shoe. Mashed potato with the consistency of wallpaper paste. Peas like painted ball bearings. I fear for my fillings and do not put anything in my mouth. I find it hard to pretend I am hungry. Eyes follow me greedily, hungrily. I do not know who amongst these people is my friend – or who is my foe. Though I am aware that the former would take a great deal more finding than the latter.

I sigh.

'This is all bullshit,' I mutter under my breath.

'Quiet, Rant!' booms a voice.

The others titter to themselves until order is restored by basilisk-like stares and hissing threats. Bastards. They'll be sorry.

From the corner of my eye I see The Pipe leave his seat at the corner table and head towards me. I have been expecting this. I am prepared, rehearsed. I breathe deeply, try to relax. Luckily no one notices, as The Pipe now has the full focus of everyone present.

The Pipe is what is known as a bit of a character. This particular character is called The Pipe because he used to beat his victims unconscious with a four-foot length of steel pipe. The Pipe would then use his pipe to break his victim's arms and legs at the knee and elbow joint. And then The Pipe would insert his pipe as far as he could into the victim's rectum. Apparently this is farther than you might think. After a judicious application of superglue, The Pipe would then attach his pipe to a high-pressure air hose such as those found in garages for inflating car tyres, and he would fill up his victims until they popped.

Some people just have a little too much time and imagination on their hands. Except when it comes to choosing nicknames, obviously.

Of course, The Pipe only did this to wrong'uns. Victims who were also villains like him. That's all right then. Although I am very aware that I am now a villain in the eyes of those around me. Oh, Lordy.

Then I become aware that he is standing behind me. I sense, rather than see, as he lunges towards me and I turn and extend my arm in one movement. Exactly as I have been taught.

The corner of the metal tray in my hand catches him across the nose and blood gushes spectacularly down the front of his prison overalls. I take this in and am amazed at how little it affects me. Of late I have become conditioned to random displays of violence in ways that I would never have imagined possible.

'Bastah!' shouts The Pipe. 'Ah'm gonna pipe you now, you shit!'

How original, I think, stepping quickly to the side as he lunges at me again. Where do they get their lines from? Cons R Us or the Mockney Muppet Mart, perhaps?

As The Pipe turns I notice that he has, as predicted, changed his weapon of choice for a homemade short knife of sorts, made from the bridge of his false teeth, sharpened and stuck into a wooden lace bobbin.

'Come 'ere, shit,' he murmurs. 'Come 'ere while I stabs you, come 'ere for a stabbin', get 'ere now while I gives you what you deserves, you shit.'

I resist the temptation to tell him that if he carries on like this he will have to change his name from The Pipe to The Shitstabber, and hold the tray out in front of me like a shield.

Then, suddenly, everything leaks away into darkness and amid the angry shouts and screams I can feel the moment slipping away. Torches flash back and forth, trying to locate the source of the problem and I know that, for the moment at least, I am no longer a part of the equation.

I leave the babble behind me as I allow myself to slip into the comforting blackness.

*Thursday May 6th. 4pm.*

It was as black as pitch down there.

The tunnels and sewerage pipes seemed to split in every direction except the one I wanted to follow. *Just keep heading downhill*, Sam had said, *and sooner or later you have to come out on the river and there are any number of outlets and pipes there.*

Simple physics. For simple people. Every branch I took seemed to lead me further and further uphill. And being a simple person, without even the simplest grasp of physics, it never occurred to me to turn around and run the other way. The downhill way. Quite apart from the fact that Bela Barbu's cronies were back there somewhere, splashing about and (presumably) uttering fruity phrases in whatever language they spoke, and that the stench in these tunnels made it extremely difficult for me to concentrate on anything beyond holding my breath, I now seemed to have reached the very bowels (as it were) of the sewerage system and every passageway seemed to lead upwards.

I had tried to shake off my pursuers but it was impossible to move silently through the cramped tunnels with any kind of speed, and they had been gaining on me steadily and relentlessly.

As I came to yet another sewer junction with no sign of an exit I paused and tried to take stock of my situation. As usual my stock and funds were low and I appeared to be in a seller's market. If I wasn't up to my neck in shit then I was certainly up to my knees in it and sinking fast.

I toyed (for all of about a second) with the idea of ducking down beneath the thick brown gloop that came up to my knees and hiding until my pursuers had passed by. But I had a feeling that they weren't going to give up that easily, and the sludge looked so thick that I could only imagine myself afloat like a greasy brown turd in a toilet, or a greasy brown American tourist on top of the Dead Sea.

My torch was beginning to flicker.

It looked as though I was going to have to make a stand of some description.

I looked down at the gun I'd liberated. Was I up to using it? As the thick splashing and cursing behind me started to grow louder, it looked like I was about to find out.

In the dying torchlight I spotted a small alcove. I stepped up into it, pushed myself back up against the wall as far as I could and switched off the torch. I had only just managed it when lights began to reflect off the surface of the water around me, giving the chamber a dull yellow glow. The sound of splashing grew louder, and dim figures, wading along in single file, began to enter from the tunnel. They had suddenly all grown quiet, as if sensing a trap of some kind; they paused less than three feet from where I cowered.

The only sound now was the constant dripping, and a rumbling noise in the distance.

There were three of them. Silently they moved to cover the three exits from the chamber. Now the only way open was the way we'd all come.

I sank down onto my hands and knees as silently as I could, until only my head was above the thick sludge. I gagged for a moment, and had to pause and close my eyes to stem a wave of giddiness and nausea.

One of my pursuers chose this moment to slip. He threw his legs into the air, performed a gymnastic manoeuvre which would probably have got him a 9.9 in the Olympics for difficulty, if only a 1.1 for execution, and fell headlong into the filth. I laughed silently, which did mean my mouth was open when the resultant wave of crap hit me. This taught me not to laugh at other people's misfortunes. Sort of.

The other two guys didn't have my insight, however, and they giggled like schoolboys at their companion, who stood up spluttering and cursing and rounded on them, shouting angrily and waving his gun around.

Whilst they were otherwise engaged, I started to creep along toward the only empty exit, pushing the briefcase ahead of me and keeping as low as possible whilst resisting the urge to spit. Or swallow. As I crept into the tunnel the shouting seemed to increase in volume, whilst the air around me seemed to grow even more thick and cloying, though I wouldn't have thought this was possible. Somewhere in the back of my mind a story popped up about the gas that builds up in sewer systems, and I started to panic that I would pass out and choke to death down here. At the moment that seemed the least of my worries, however, and I slowly turned to check out how my followers were doing.

They seemed to be fighting among themselves quite happily now, and I started pushing myself along backwards through the muck away from them. The freestyle diver lashed out and punched one of the others in the face, knocking him into the grim stream that flowed around his knees. Needless to say, this isn't one of the recommendations in *How to Make Friends and Influence People*; he came up spluttering and screaming blue murder, in between bouts of puking. The third guy thought this was all too much and started slapping his knees and laughing uproariously. The other two rounded on him menacingly, and he managed to stifle the laughing, but even I could hear him snottering out a few giggles. They started to advance on him, muttering something that could only be taken as a serious threat to his manhood, even if you didn't understand the lingo. Which I didn't. So of course they could have been asking for a cuddle and a wet wipe, but somehow I doubt it. Mr Clean straightened up and said something threatening right back, and clonked Mr Pukeymouth with his torch, buying himself enough time to pull out his gun.

I had been quite enjoying this exchange, slowly distancing myself from it and finding myself about twenty feet away now. It was becoming more like watching a film or television. With smell-surround. When the gun appeared, though, I suddenly found myself wanting to stand up and shout, 'Excuse me, but I've done the gun-shooting-in-enclosed-spaces-with-gaseous-emissions and really, trust me, it's not big or clever and does nothing for tonsorial elegance.' Fortunately my fear of being shot was greater than my fear of being theoretically blown to smithereens, so I kept my mouth shit—sorry, *shut*. For which I am truly grateful.

For, as you have by no doubt guessed, Mr Clean pulled his trigger and fired a shot into the roof of the chamber. The only thing that happened at this point is that Mr Olympic Diver and Mr Pukeymouth dived back into the primordial slime from whence they came. When they surfaced, both were holding their own pocket cannons and looking for something to fill with holes.

I started back-pedalling furiously, no longer worried about the noise. It was pretty unlikely they'd hear me over their own racket, anyway.

The weaving torches and the muzzle flashes from the guns gave the whole scene a kind of strobing effect, and I watched in horror as the three of them jerked back and forth around the tiny chamber. Then Mr Pukeymouth plunged into the tunnel I was in, firing one last shot over his shoulder as he dived headlong, and landed with a splat and the sound of thick, plopping bubbles.

I finally panicked a bit too much and lost my footing on the greasy bricks beneath me as I pushed backwards. My head slipped under the flowing river of poop. For a second I was blinded by the thick liquid as it flowed into my ears, eyes and nose, and then the world seemed illuminated once more as the gloop around me contracted, sending me shooting down the passageway like a foot into a well-oiled sea boot.

I halted abruptly at the next sharp bend by cunningly jamming my head into the brick wall and cushioning the impact with my neck and shoulder muscles. I floated there for a few seconds, trying to gather my thoughts – you know the sort of thing: *Where am I? What's my name? What is the principal export of Madagascar? What the fuck happened to my spine?* Then I sucked in the enticing aroma of burned crap and it all came flooding back to me. It's coffee and vanilla, I think. The principal export of Madagascar, not the smell. The other details were still a little fuzzy to me.

I gazed back down the tunnel in the direction I thought I'd come from, but there was nothing but blackness. I couldn't hear anything, but that could have been the combined effect of having been at the centre of my fourth explosion in less than two days and having my ears stuffed with prime quality people-manure.

I stood up shakily. I was having great difficulty straightening my back out properly, but I think a burly blacksmith with a trouser press and a steamroller would have had trouble straightening my back out just at that moment, so I made the best of it and struggled along, like a puppet Quasimodo made out of cack, into the gloom. At least the ground under my feet seemed to be falling at last.

Somewhere ahead I could hear the sound of traffic and I instinctively followed it – pausing only to clean some of the gloop out of my ears – taking a few wrong turns and backtracking as the sound gradually increased.

Eventually I walked full length into a steel ladder and, once I had got my faculties back, I peered upwards through the gloom. There seemed to be dim light filtering down through a manhole cover.

Cautiously, I began to climb.

About halfway up there was a crawl space. Unsure of where exactly I would be surfacing, I decided the wise option would be to hide the case and the gun, then try to climb out without attracting too much attention. Not the easiest of tasks, granted, given my physical state, but at least it would give me an air of victimhood rather than armed lunacy. Incriminating items stashed, I continued climbing and, after much struggling and swearing, lifted the heavy cover off.

I peered around, trying to figure out where in London I'd managed to escape to. I was hoping to have put as much distance between Barbu's goons and myself as possible.

The building in front of me did look strangely familiar, and I tried to rack my knowledge of London landmarks to figure out where it…

…Oh.

I was gazing at the façade of the sewerage works.

I debated whether to sink back out of sight, but I knew that I could spend the rest of my life wandering around down there in Pooland without finding another exit.

Everything seemed quiet. The minibus was gone, as were the high-end cars and limousines that had been here when we arrived. So, Sam and Co. had abandoned me and fled with their share of the loot, or whatever it was, the police had disappeared, presumably in pursuit of someone, and the villains had gone to ground.

In all, it wasn't a bad result.

All I had to do now was

get to a phone

call up Anna's captors

clean myself up, then

avoid the police

and a bunch of gangsters

and the C.I.A

and presumably anyone else the Government could find to hunt me down and claim the price on my scalp (MI5, anyone? The Olympic Ballroom team?), then

make the trade and get Anna back without either of us being killed, arrested or maimed.

Easy.

Oh, and

find a way to get out of the country, after

persuading Anna of the truth of my story without being killed, arrested or maimed.

Not so easy.

I climbed slowly out of my hidey-hole, looking around as I went. Everything was silent. I pulled the manhole cover back and dropped it back into place as quietly and carefully as I could. Which meant, of course, that it clanged like the bells of hell in the silent car park and trapped my fingers under the edge.

I was still squeaking and panting and trying to free myself when I felt something cold touch the back of my neck.

'Well, Mr Rant, we meet again,' said a familiar voice.

There was the click of a gun being cocked.

'Hello,' I said. 'Pardon me if…ooh…I don't get up. Fingers, see. Drain. Hurts. Could you…er…?'

The crack across the back of my skull helped obliterate the pain.

And everything else.

## SCENE TWELVE
## MY ACHY BREAKY PARTS

*Thursday May 6th. Evening.*

I was tied to a rickety steel chair.

Naked.

But at least I was clean now, much to everyone's relief – not least mine. God only knew what diseases I might be harbouring after my time in the flotation tank of the London sewerage system (though at this moment in time my chances of living to see them flourish are extremely slim), but the first thing Mr Barbu had his henchmen do after we arrived here was to strip me down and clean me off with a high-pressure fire hose. What was left of my skin was pink and shiny and smelt of Parma Violets.

We were in a large open space that looked as though it had been a garage at one point, though it was obviously long abandoned. There were oil-stains on the floor and oddly shaped, uncared-for tools lying around.

Speaking of oddly shaped, uncared-for tools, the three men in the room with me were still and silent.

I tried to make conversation but they weren't having any of it.

'Look,' I said, 'if you're going to torture me and give me a long, lingering death, just tell me now so I can have a heart attack and get it over with. I'm feeling a bit tingly down my left arm as it is.'

Nothing.

'Hello?' I said. 'Listen, I don't know anything, so you're wasting your time and energy. So unless this is some strange audition for an advert for the newest line in Trabant cars or some weird late night version of *Punk'd*, then maybe you could just let me go and we'll say no more about it. Hmmm? Promise I won't tell on you.'

Still nothing for a few moments. Then the man in the middle, Bela Barbu, nodded slightly.

The other two started towards me.

*Uh-oh*, I thought.

At first they flicked wet towels at me, which hurt like a bastard, let me tell you.

Then one of them came over and punched me in the jaw. I felt a molar loosen. Tasted blood.

Then the other one punched me in the stomach.

Then they took turns standing on my toes with their heavy boots.

Then they took turns whacking me round the head with rolled-up newspapers, which hurts more than you might think.

Then they do-si-doed their partners and hooked me up to a car battery and a set of alligator clips on my nipples. The battery was flat, which disappointed them enormously, but it really stung anyway. My nipples were standing out like chapel hat pegs.

My heart attack eluded me. Though I did learn how to yodel, which is some small consolation.

Then one of them grabbed my shoulders and shook me really hard.

I was plagued by the image of my brain bouncing around like a pea in a whistle. *What happens,* I wondered, *if I end up with some terrible brain injury that leaves me fluent in Turkish but unable to toilet myself?*

Barbu sat silently through it all on a chair opposite me, pecking away at a laptop, occasionally printing things off or moving his legs to avoid water or blood splatters. He did not seem in the least concerned or interested in what was going on.

Throughout everything I didn't let any useful information slip, though this was not for the want of trying. All I managed to say was *ow, ooyah, ouch, aaaaaaah, stopitstopitstopit you bastards, not the testicles, owowow, gnnnnnaaarrrggghhh,* and *I'll tell you anything you want to know just don't hurt me any more, please.* Though not necessarily in that order. Things are a little fuzzy in my recollection of this time.

I must have lost consciousness at some point, since I suddenly found myself jerking awake as a bucket of icy water was thrown over me. I closed my eyes and tried to will myself into a coma but hands started slapping at my face.

'Should we give him an anti-Semitic?' a voice asked.

'Not just yet,' came back Bela Barbu's voice. 'I think Mr Rant is ready to talk now, hmmm?'

I opened an eye.

I couldn't help myself. 'What's an anti-Semitic?'

Barbu smiled.

'A speciality of Eugene's,' he said, while I'm thinking, *Eugene?* You can't be a hired killer and torturer with a name like Eugene. It's worse than Eustace. Not much, I'll admit, but worse all the same. Though what you'd have to go through at school would be enough to turn anyone into a sociopath.

'It involves cutting away the penis and testicles with the bluntest instrument you can find to do the job and leaving only the foreskin attached by a thin piece of flesh. It is, of course, done without anaesthetic and I'm led to believe that it is extremely painful and time consuming. Though in your case I do not think it would take so long. More of a minor operation from what I can see.'

'Hey,' I whimpered, 'it's cold in here with no clothes on.'

'Whatever,' Barbu said. 'Would you like to try it anyway?'

'Maybe later,' I replied, all the while thinking that if Eugene didn't do it, Anna probably would. Or at the very least she'd offer to hold me down.

'It's a bit racist though, isn't it?' I said, hoping to cause a distraction (though if he wasn't distracted by the sight of my naked booty, then talking wasn't going to help).

'What's racist?' he asked.

'Calling it an anti-Semitic.

'How so?'

'Well...racial stereotyping and all that.'

'An interesting point. My Grandmother was Jewish, on my father's side, so I am in fact myself one quarter Jewish.'

'Ah...' I said, knowingly, 'the old "one cannot be racist against one's own racial group" line. But isn't it dependent on your audience? Should one only say such things to one's own race and social group? Because only then can one be sure that the humour you project is taken in the manner in which it is given.'

'But Barthes would argue that such an assumption regarding the other's ability to separate the signifiers you use to convey your point of view from the signified would in itself be racist, would he not, Mr Rant?'

'I'd need to think about it. I was thinking more of Bernard Manning's arguments myself, and they never convinced me.'

'Okay, for now we'll just call it filleting your cock. How does that suit?'

'It'll hurt just as much either way, won't it?'

'I sincerely hope so,' said Barbu. 'But like I said, I do not think it will be necessary. I think you are ready to cooperate, and we do not have all night.'

'Okay,' I said. 'Shoot.' Barbu picked up some papers and a gun from the floor and stood. Walked over me to me.

'Er, bad choice of words,' I said. 'Ask anything you like. Anything.'

He leant over me. Raised the gun. Then took a quick step backwards.

'What is that smell?' he gasped.

'Sorry. I'm getting a little stressed here.'

He spent a couple of seconds wafting his hands around theatrically and then came back over to me, though not quite so close this time.

'Who sent you here?' he asked quietly, breathing through his mouth. 'Who was it that sent you to kill me? Do you even know?'

'No,' I muttered.

He considered this for a few seconds. He knew that I was broken, that I was unlikely to lie to him. 'Tell me what you know about...' he checked some papers in his hand, '...Samuel Smith.'

'He told me he's a CIA agent. Semi-retired. Him and his cronies set up this whole thing. To catch people who employed the service of assassins.'

'And you believe that?'

I no longer knew what to believe. 'Shouldn't I?' I asked.

He observed me again. Almost – I would think, if I didn't know better – almost sadly.

'I think you know nothing about what is going on. I think you're a fool who has been sucked into this game and used. And I think you are of no use to me whatsoever.'

'Well at least we agree on something,' I said. 'Can I go now, only I've got a bus to catch and it gets busy at the emergency department when the pubs kick out.'

'Still joking. I like that. Now, before I kill you,' he said quietly, 'there is something I would like you to see.'

He dropped a glossy black-and-white photograph into my lap. It showed a young man in a double-breasted suit and a trilby hat, smoking a cheroot and grinning. He looked like Flash Harry in the St. Trinian's films. But there was no doubt that I was looking at a much younger version of Samuel Smith.

I felt my heart sinking. I didn't want to hear what Barbu was about to say.

Over Sam's shoulder, just visible, was a rundown public house; the name above the door read THE KHAZGINJYSTANIA ARMS HOTEL.

Oh dear.

'This is a photograph of a gentleman who goes by the name of William Milligan, a.k.a. Billy the Pill, a.k.a. the Rumour Mill. And I suppose, for now, a.k.a. Samuel Smith. He is wanted for questioning by the police in several European countries but he is something of a slippery character. He is not, as you seem to think, an American. He was born in London and has been a dealer of some significance since the nineteen fifties. He is a conman.'

My heart still stubbornly carried on beating, but it sank still further. Any lower and I could use it as a cushion to keep my buttocks off this bloody cold chair.

Odd snippets of conversation replayed in my head.

*So do you think he knows?*

*Not yet, but pretty soon...and then we have a problem.*

*And dealing with that problem?*

'It's just a con?' I said. 'This is just about money.'

'It is always about money, Mr Rant.'

'And what about the others? Joshua. Sebastian. Abigail?'

'The others are members of his gang.'

As he spoke he flicked more photographs in front of me, all of them showing younger versions of the GIA.

'Joshua Smith, a.k.a. Benjamin Cooper, a.k.a. the Chicken Coop, a.k.a. Benny the Answer Phone. Started out as a pimp and then got into the import and export business – people, not goods. Word on the street has it that a rival pimp poked out his voice box with a snooker cue. Cooper was taken to hospital and patched up, then returned to the snooker hall and finished off the game he was playing – apparently using his rival's testicles in lieu of a cue ball.

'Mr Van Gogh, a.k.a. St. John Raleigh-Ramsbottom, a.k.a. The Professor, a.k.a. The Radge from the Raj. Something of an entrepreneur, this chap, and very well connected, it would seem. He set up a somewhat lucrative opium trade when he was in India in the forties, just before the British pulled out, and has been overseeing it ever since. He apparently supplies about forty percent of the Scottish heroin market – which is a lot of money.

'The other two I do not know, but I am assuming they are probably associates, or just plain bodyguards, brought in to help them run this latest gig. Together the big three have masterminded some of the biggest extortion rackets, big cons, and long games in history. Rumour has it that they were the first crew to sell London Bridge to an American collector.'

'I just wanted to save my wife,' I pleaded. 'And my child. Though I didn't know about the child when this all started. I thought this Sam whatever-his-name-is was trying to help. I thought he was just helping me to rescue my wife. Please, you have to believe me.'

'I do believe you, Mr Rant. And don't get too down. You weren't to know; he is very, very good at what he does. He has been scamming people for a long, long time. And the good conman has no room for sentimentality. He didn't care about you or anyone else. So remember – because of this man you will soon be dead, and so will your wife.'

He watched me closely.

'I can help you to get your property back,' I said, desperately, 'I know where one of the cases is and—what?'

He was laughing, still with that same sad smile.

'I doubt very much that you know anything of the sort,' he said. 'And besides – the contents of that case will be useless by this time tomorrow. Don't make the same mistake that Mr Milligan—sorry, Mr *Smith* made. There is always a back-up plan, and copies can be made.'

'Copies of what? The title deeds to a sewerage works? What use are they to Sam, or whatever he's called, if they've been signed and authorized?'

He laughed again. 'Your ignorance really does astound me, Mr Rant. I cannot believe how totally you have been duped by these people.'

'Join the club,' I said. 'Look. As you keep telling me, I have no idea at all what this is all about. Just let me go and try to save my wife, at least. You can follow me if you want, try to get the bastards who set you up…'

He had been shaking his head throughout my pleas. 'No, Mr Rant.'

'But even if it is a con,' I said, 'they still have to collect on the deal – I just need to call the people who set you up and arrange—'

'Tell me, Mr Rant, how much were these people offering you for the retrieval of the briefcase?'

'One hundred thousand. All together. Fifty for killing you and fifty for the case… So you see you'll get one of the cases back and I can even give you the money, too, if you like. And I have a little extra that I…er…borrowed…'

He was laughing heartily now, as was everyone else in the room.

'Oh, now, Mr Rant. I think you'll find that the contents of those briefcases are worth a little more than that on the open market. And Mr Milligan will certainly be aware of their value. He will not go anywhere near our Romanian friends. He will be off to find richer pickings. I will catch up with him sooner or later, don't you worry.'

'But I can help you—'

'No,' he states, with finality. 'No, Mr Rant. You are nothing but a liability now. This is not some corny spy film where the arch villain spills his wicked plans to you and then, by some miraculous turn of events, allows you to go free and save the day. This is not an action movie with you as the romantic lead. This is business, Mr Rant. And nothing gets in the way of business.'

He raised the gun and pressed it against my forehead.

I closed my eyes.

'Please,' I said. 'Please.'

'Any last words, Mr Rant?'

Nothing came, nothing except, 'I'm sorry, Anna.'

'How touching. Goodbye, Mr Rant.'

I felt him cock the gun.

I held my breath.

I waited for the explosion and darkness.

All I heard was a ringing sound in my ears.

*Is that it?* I thought. *Is that all I get?*

The ringing continued.

I carefully opened my eyes and squinted, cross-eyed, at Barbu's finger on the trigger as he dug in his jacket pocket. He lifted a mobile to his ear with a curt greeting, and then listened.

I watched his finger tighten on the trigger.

He said something quietly, and then disconnected the call. I was still staring at his trigger finger, which had gone white. The slightest twitch, and… I carried on holding my breath, though there were now spots swimming in front of my eyes from lack of oxygen.

I frowned, wondering what the delay was, and tried not to flinch as the gun dug deeper into my forehead.

There was a long, long pause as I watched Barbu try to get a grip on himself. He walked across the room, screamed, kicked out at a pile of rubbish that was lying there, gnashed his feet and stamped his teeth. Or something like that. If I didn't know better, I'd say he was a tad miffed at something.

He came back over and pushed the gun into my forehead again. His finger tightened and loosened, tightened – and then he seemed to gain control, taking deep breaths.

Eventually, he hissed, 'Well. It would seem that we have something of a problem, Mr Rant.'

We?

I cleared my throat, and blurted out, 'What kind of a problem I mean if there's any way I can help you know I'll do all that I can the case is yours after all so let's go get it anything to be of service just tell me what you need I know we can work well together what's the story morning glory?'

I sucked in a breath before I passed out and was about to start in again when he said, 'It would appear that my office at home has been… breached. Certain files were deleted or stolen and my safe has been emptied. Your Mr Milligan has indeed been cleverer than I thought.'

I gulped. It was louder than I thought it would be, causing Barbu and his bodyguards to jump and look around. Barbu glared at me.

'Sorry,' I said.

'This being the case,' he continued, lowering the gun, 'it would seem that you and your friends—'

'No friends of mine,' I said, 'hate them, and hate them, nasty men. And woman. Ptoooee.'

I spat. We both looked at the gob on his nice Gucci shoes.

'Sorry,' I said again, whilst one of the bodyguards rushed forwards and wiped it off with his hanky.

'…it would seem that you and your colleagues—'

'Not my coll—'

'Shut up!'

Up I shut. The bodyguard slapped me across the head for good measure. It was quite a gentle slap, considering, but they had to pick me and my chair up off the floor before Barbu could continue.

'Now. It would seem that you and your *colleagues,*' – he glared at me for a moment but I kept shtum – 'that you now have something which is of the utmost value to me. Now, I know that you can supply some of what I need. And it would appear that the only lead we have left to one half of the goods is our Romanian friends.'

He looked at me, obviously wanting some kind of response.

'Uh-huh,' I said.

'And it would appear that you are our primary contact with them, as they are obviously expecting a call from you in the near future.'

'Yup,' I said.

'And if you were to assist me in this matter, I might be able to see my way to rescuing your wife.'

'Uh-huh.'

'And perhaps Mr Milligan will consider selling…some part of the collection to them anyway. As we have already established, this is all about money, and from what I can gather, Billy the Pill is a very greedy man. And more importantly, the Romanians must have some contact information for him. So if nothing else, I have the feeling that Mr Milligan will want to tie up some loose ends and make sure that there is no chain of evidence that leads back to him.'

*Collection? Goods?* I thought. 'Mm-hmmm,' I said.

Barbu waited.

'Well?' he asked.

I let him stew for a couple of seconds, while my mind tried to process this latest turn of events. Perhaps, at long last, events were beginning to turn in my favour. I needed to take advantage. How to play this? Then suddenly I had it. Gathering my last reserves of energy and trying desperately to ignore the pain, I summoned up the spirit of Vinnie Jones. I gave a crooked smile and looked Barbu in the eyes.

'Hmmm. It would appear that the shoe is on the other foot now.'

'Pardon?' said Barbu.

'Well,' I said, realising that I did indeed have the upper hand, or foot, or whatever. 'Say please at least.'

'*Pardon?*' said Barbu.

'Say please. I mean, it's the least you could do. After all, it would appear that you now need me to help you. After all this shit, you seem to think that you just have to snap your fingers and I'll do exactly as you ask. I'll run along and get the briefcase I hid, then toddle off and set up the men who stole, or wanted to steal, whatever it is you're hawking. Where do you get off, anyway? Some bunch of cheap crooks running around trying to get one up on another bunch of cheap crooks, torturing people, kidnapping people, lying, cheating...thinking you're some kind of royalty because you can extort or beat money out of people. Maybe you're going to have to convince me why it's in my best interest to help you anyway. What? Cat got your tongue?'

He looked at me long and hard. *Got you now,* I thought. *Pricked your conscience at last.* They're like casting directors. Sometimes all it takes with these people is to show them that you're not impressed with their pathetic little schemes and they fold like a director at the BBC who's been shown the ratings for ITV's latest reality show.

I know what you're thinking. I should've just gone along with whatever they wanted, got Anna back, let them fight it out amongst themselves, gone home, tended my wounds and got on with my life. All I can say in my defence is that I was tired and emotional after my time with these people, and my mouth seemed to be running off on its own. Though, as you've probably gathered by now, I don't need the excuse of extended periods of torture and pressure to succumb to verbal diarrhoea.

And Vinnie Jones?

'Come on,' I said, 'let's see you grovel. Who's the daddy now?'

A moment more of silence, then,

'Eugene,' said Barbu.

Eugene didn't answer, just stood to attention.

'I think now might be a good moment to give Mr Rant an anti-Semitic.' He paused. *'Please.'*

Oops. Me and my big gob.

Within seconds I went from Vinnie Jones to Corporal Jones.

'Whoa,' I shouted, 'let's not panic. Just hold on a sec—'

'No, Mr Rant, you are quite right. After all of the abuse that my employees and I have put you through I am sure that you will need a great deal of convincing that it is in your best interests to help us. But let's see now, all we really need is your voice on a telephone to set up the meeting, and some directions to the other briefcase. It does not matter if you speak in a slightly higher register than usual. See you in a little while, Mr Rant.' He turned back to Eugene. 'Make it slow. And make sure you keep him alive. For the moment.'

And with that, he left.

I tried calling after him but there was no response and a few seconds later the steel door clanged shut.

*Well,* I thought, *at least it's only two against one now. The odds are definitely getting better.*

Eugene walked to a table in the corner of the room and picked up a rather rusty old pair of wire cutters and a cross-headed screwdriver. I tried desperately to cross my legs, but they were securely fastened to the chair. My bottom seemed to have gone strangely dormant, my sphincter so tightly puckered that only the tiniest trump managed to sneak out, with a sound probably only dogs could hear. Just when I needed my deadliest defence, too.

'Okay, Barbu,' I shouted, as loud as I could. 'You win, you've convinced me. I'm sorry I had a go at you. You can call off the boys now. You've had your fun. Ha ha hahaha! Very good. Barbu? Mr Barbu? Sir? Barbu! Ow, ow, *owwww,* get off me you dirty bastard. Aaaaaaaarrrggghhh—! *Oooooh.*'

This last was because, after grabbing a handful of flesh, Eugene had succeeded in (quite gently, I thought) inserting the screwdriver down my urethra and was using it to hold my Right Honourable Member for Piddlington out straight. He now held the wire cutters in his other hand and was studying said member the way my father used to eye up the Sunday roast, before laying into it with a fork and carving knife and ripping it into unrecognizable chunks.

I vaguely heard the sound of a car pulling away outside, and realized that there wasn't going to be any reprieve.

'Eugene,' I said, in my best menacing Alan Rickman voice – though it wasn't that convincing, even to me. I don't think he uses quite so much vibrato when he does it. 'Eugene, think about this. You could be in very serious trouble if you do this. Now, if you let me go, I promise I'll put in a good word for you with the police and – now, Eugene, don't do that! Careful with those wire-cutters, Eugene! *Eugene!*'

The wire cutters felt cold as he slid them around my gender-defining bits, and I suddenly found myself beyond words.

'Say goodbye to Mr Rant Junior,' said Eugene, smiling.

'Bye, bye,' I squeaked, like Sweep saying farewell to Mr Corbett. There was a tear or two in my eyes at the thought of being parted from my lifelong companion. 'Bye, bye.'

Reflexively, I went for my last line of defence.

And threw up on Eugene's head.

He stepped back, disgusted, and walked over to the table to mop himself down with a somewhat unsanitary towel. I could see him considering the value of obeying his orders and keeping me alive. He must have been sorely tempted to just finish me off then.

He started back towards me, and from the look in his eyes he definitely meant business. And as far as I was concerned, business was not good.

Then the lights went out.

I sat as still as I could, the cold steel still pinching at my parts, as all around me a series of snaps, crackles and pops led me to believe that heaven (or maybe hell) is a bowl of cereal.

I just had time to register a thick, sickly smell that caught in the back of my throat and made me want to cough (and I really wasn't in a position to start coughing) before I found myself being dragged backwards across the floor on the chair. I peered into the gloom over my shoulder but everything was misty and my eyes were beginning to water.

As we neared the door, the light from outside backlit a gas masked figure as I was dragged, bumping, over the step. (Aren't screwdrivers a lot *bigger* than you would think when you hold one in your hand?) I squeaked with relief as the wire cutters came loose and fell away, hoping against hope that nothing else had fallen away with them.

# SCENE THIRTEEN
# THE NAKED TRUTH

*Friday May 7$^{th}$. Shortly after midnight.*

I was bundled into the back of a transit van by my rescuers, still tied to the chair and still naked. The doors slammed before I could ask what was going on and we sped off.

We rattled along the road a ways, taking a few turns at random, obviously attempting to throw off any pursuit. I heard the engine turned off and a few seconds later the back doors opened.

A man climbed into the back with me I regarded him upside down. He looked familiar... Yes! It was the policeman from the sewage works! The Scottish one.

I breathed a sigh of relief. 'Thank God,' I said, 'I was beginning to wonder who'd gotten hold of me this time. Can you untie me please? Bit chilly in the back here.'

'No' just yet, Mr Rant. We'll need tae be away again in jist a jiffy. Ah jist wanted tae ask whit yae did wi' thi sootcase. Huv thu still goat it at the warehoose? Huv *you* goat it? We couldnae find it.'

'No,' I said, 'I've hidden it up my arse. Of course I don't have it. I hid it in the sewers by the sewage works. We can go and pick it up if you untie me.'

'Jist tell me where—'

'No. I have been tied naked to a chair for hours, beaten, humiliated, and then dragged out into the night with a screwdriver up me pongo. I'm saying nothing until you untie me and give me something to wear.'

He gazed at me thoughtfully for a second and then acquiesced. When I was free he watched, wincing, as I delicately pulled the tool from my tool. We both sighed with relief when I'd finished. Then he reluctantly handed me his overcoat.

'I'll give it you back as soon as—'

'Nae, laddie,' he said, looking a little bit nauseous, 'You keep it.'

I noticed he was careful not to touch me as he loosened the ropes and handed the coat over. I didn't smell that bad, did I? Well, come to think of it, I did – but it was nothing compared to earlier.

'Thank you,' I said, wholeheartedly. 'Who are you?'

'Name's Mallefant, Inspector Mallefant.

'Pleased to meet you, Inspector,' I said, holding out my hand.

He gazed at it for a moment, then pulled out a pack of sterile wipes, slipped one from the packet and wrapped it around his own hand. Then he shook mine, looking uneasy.

'Aye, nice tae make yer acquaintance, likesay.'

What a strange little man.

'Come away up and sit in the front,' he said.

We climbed out of the van and walked to the passenger door. As I opened it I saw Ms Agent Smith sitting behind the wheel. I screamed. It was a manly, hero-who's-been-through-the-wars kind of scream, but a scream none the less.

'Whisht, laddie,' hissed Mallefant. 'They might still be in the area. Whit's up with you?'

'It's…her!' I said, pointing. 'She's…one of them!'

'Aye, Ah ken that,' he said.

'Well, arrest her!' I shouted.

'Well, liking other lassies is no' a criminal offence these days. She cannae help the way she is.'

'No,' I shout at him, 'She's with them – the bad guys. Well, when I say the bad guys, they're kind of the good guys compared to the other bad guys, but they're still bad guys compared to likes of, say, you and me, though I admit I've done some things that might make other people think I'm a bit of a bad guy, but I'm sure if you let me explain then you'll understand I'm a good-ish kind of a guy. Unless...you're a not-quite-so-bad guy...and you're working with...the good...the bad... the...'

I could feel my voice, my body and my entire system of thought and logic giving up on me as the sentence faded away. I let out a strangled sob and sat down on the pavement.

'Rant, calm down,' said Ms Agent Smith. 'This man is a bona fide police officer and he's here to help us. I was trying to track down what was going down with Sam Smith and his cronies – I work for the Secret Service. And this man is my uncle Menzies. Menzies Mallefant.

We're trying to help you. We are the good guys.'

'The *good* good guys or the *bad* good guys?'

'Rant, it doesn't matter right now. We're all you've got. Or we can leave you out here in a coat and nothing else and your wife and child will be dead by this evening.'

It was a fair point. Resignedly I climbed into the cab of the van. Mallefant climbed in after me, being careful to first lay down some antiseptic wipes on the seat, and making sure no part of him touched me as he sat down next to me. He kept his hand over his mouth the whole time. Some people are just plain rude, don't you think?

I directed them to the manhole cover I'd escaped from and Ms Agent Smith climbed down and up in no time, carrying the suitcase and my gun as though they weighed nothing. She didn't even break a sweat or wince at the smell that came off the suitcase. It must be a lesbian thing; my eyes were watering even before she opened the rear doors and threw the case into the back of the van. And Mallefant looked like he wanted to run screaming into the night. He pulled out a paper face mask and slipped it on.

'My place or yours?' said Ms Agent Smith.

'My place is two hundred miles north of here,' I told her.

'I wasn't talking to you,' she said to me. 'Uncle?'

We both looked at him. What little we could see of his face was a mask of horror.

'My place it is then,' she said.

For the rest of the journey I didn't bother to speak to him or answer his questions. The combination of the mask and the accent made it impossible to understand him. And Ms Agent Smith was too busy driving to talk, so I let myself slip into sleep.

When I woke up we were outside a very nice block of flats next to the river. Agent Smith grabbed the case and hustled me inside, with Mallefant bringing up the rear, watching the street in case we'd somehow been followed.

I was dead on my feet. Everything hurt. Even saying *ow* hurt. I was more hurt than a Newcastle fan when they were relegated out of the premiership and Sunderland stayed up. (Well, maybe not quite *that* hurt.)

'Why don't you lie down?' Ms Agent Smith asked. 'You look done in.'

I nodded and waddled off in search of a bedroom. At the door, I paused. 'By the way, what happened to Agent Smith? The boy one. I saw him get shot at the sewage works.'

'He took a round in the shoulder, but he's going to be fine. We got him to the hospital pretty quickly.'

'Didn't they ask awkward questions?'

'Took him to an Army hospital. They're used to that kind of thing.'

I supposed they were.

I went down a short corridor and found a bedroom, I think. There was no bed in it so I just I lay down on the floor but, though I dozed on and off, I couldn't sleep. Every time I got close and could feel my battered and bruised body gratefully succumbing to unconsciousness I kept thinking about Anna, and I jerked awake, and my body was in no fit state to be jerking, if you see what I mean. Anna. How was I going to help her now? If Ms Agent Smith had turned against the others then we were out of the loop. Would Sam and Co. really care whether she lived or died? According to Barbu they were only in it for the money.

And if Barbu was lying then they were only in it for King and Country. Or whatever it was that Americans got into it for. President and State or something. Rock and Roll. Peanut butter and jelly... I jerked awake again. Whimpered.

I wished Anna was here. *Come back, Anna,* I thought, *even if it's only to kill me for the mess I've gotten us into. Come back and dead me, don't be dead.* Awake again. Ow.

The Romanians could be anywhere, and only they knew where the meet would be, and Sam had their contact details. Showaddywaddy, where are you now? I could phone their agent. I could phone my agent. I could phone Ms Agent Smith and she could come and get me…?

I jerked awake once more. It was only then that a thought occurred to me.

I got up and went back through into the living room, walking like the scarecrow in *The Wizard of Oz.* I found Ms Agent Smith and Mallefant bent over a laptop computer.

'How did you know where I was?' I asked.

'Transponder,' she said, still staring at the computer screen. It seemed to have them both transfixed.

'Oh,' I said. 'What's a transponder?'

'Tiny radio,' she said distractedly, 'I injected it into your arm last night at the safe house after I'd given you the painkiller. So we could keep tabs on you.'

'You mean I've been chipped? Like a mangy dog?'

'You said it.'

'Isn't that an invasion of my human rights?' I screeched. Or probably squeaked. I didn't have the energy to screech.

'Saved your life, didn't it?'

I couldn't argue with that. The issue of whether it had been worthwhile seemed a little less clear.

'What are you looking at?' I asked, and went over to join them.

On the screen, two men and a woman were indulging in what I can only describe as a lewd act. Lewd and loud. Surely they couldn't be watching porn together, an uncle and niece? How disgusting was that? And the quality really wasn't that great. I debated whether to sneak out and pretend I hadn't seen anything when the action on screen got even more disturbing. And up close and personal.

'Isn't that...' I couldn't finish my sentence, I was so distracted.

'The principal undersecretary of the Health Minister, yes,' said Ms Agent Smith.

'I was going to say "illegal",' I managed to get out.

'Believe me,' said Mallefant, his voice managing to convey both how appalled he was, and the undying admiration he felt for a man of such advanced years moving so gymnastically, 'this is tame compared tae what's on most of these disks.'

'Are these from Barbu?' I asked.

'Aye, they are indeed,' said Mallefant.

'So it was just about porn,' I said, sadly shaking my head. 'And fairly low grade gonzo porn at that. What is the world coming to?'

'This isnae just porn, laddie,' he said, smiling for the first time since I'd met him. 'This is dynamite. Nah, no' even that. This is a bloody great atomic bomb that's goin' tae blow the kecks off this Government.'

I closed my eyes, almost too tired and definitely in too much pain to care.

'Tell me,' I said.

So they told me. I didn't believe them. So they told me again. I still didn't believe them so they showed me. And believe me, dear reader, had I been wearing kecks at that point they would have been well and truly blown off.

'Tell me more,' I said.

It went something like this.

Mr Barbu wanted to make money. Lots of money. He was planning to take over the governance of Romania, his adopted country and private bank, but in order to do this he needed lots and lots of capital.

His plan (and it was probably only the tip of the iceberg) was to get this money by buying all of the land, on which the Olympics would take place, for a song. Compulsory purchase orders for old, unusable land that nobody had wanted for decades. At rock-bottom prices.

*How would a foreign national with no obvious stake in the Olympics manage to do this?* I hear you ask.

Well, in the good old fashioned way that politicians and the well-to-do have achieved it since time immemorial. By blackmail and corruption.

What he had amassed, on the disks we now possessed, was incriminating footage of members of every department of Government, every police force in the land, every branch of the media – in short, everyone who had any power to naysay what he was attempting to do.

And he had let them know. And had let them know that there was more than one copy. All those hundreds of people in positions of power, caught in positions of weakness.

He had gathered his footage from highly encrypted sites within the CIA, MI5, MI6, the FBI, Interpol and the vaults of the late lamented *News of the World*. His minions had hacked into every one and made copies of every person of import who was ever caught on camera or on tape committing naughtiness.

But today the CIA, having distracted him by disrupting his little gathering at the sewage works, had managed to hack him right back and had stolen or corrupted every computer network that he had access to.

'So we really are sitting on the only copies he had left?' I said, rubbing my hands with glee.

'Well,' said Ms Agent Smith, 'we're sitting on one half of it. Sam Smith has the other half.'

'But,' I continued, 'just think what we could do with this. We could get the government, the police, to mobilise everything they've got to find my wife.'

I resisted the urge to add that we could make ourselves rich beyond our wildest dreams. I was using the "noble" motivation for my character and I think it went across rather well. My audience was moved.

'Well, laddie,' said Mallefant, sadly, 'Ah'm afraid we cannae dae that. Much as Ah'd like tae see some of they numpties brought low, we've the national interest tae think of, ken? This hes tae stay between us. Naebody can know.'

'But,' I whimpered, 'Anna...'

'We've still a chance to get to Anna,' said Ms Agent Smith, consolingly. 'Sam doesn't know I'm working for someone else. He thinks I'm on their side still. I'll let him know that I've captured you and other suitcase. I'll tell him we're in on the deal and we'll arrange to go to the meeting – as far as I know he still intends to sell his half to the Romanians. That way we'll get everyone who knows about this in one fell swoop.'

'And if Sam doesn't go for it?' I asked.

'Then we follow the transponder I put in Joshua's chair.'

'Well, aren't you the sneaky one,' I said

'I have my moments,' she said, and I'm sure she blushed, just a little.

'So we go to the police?' I asked.

‘Of course,’ said Ms Agent Smith. ‘Uncle Menzies, in case you’re forgetting, is a policeman, so he’ll see to that.’

‘But how do we get them there without letting everyone know what’s in the suitcases? I thought we had to keep this all secret.’

‘Aye but, laddie,’ said Mallefant, ‘we huv a secret weapon. A real honey pot. Somethin’ that ivery police officer in the country is desperate tae get their hands on right aboot now.’

‘And what’s that?’ I asked, though in truth I already knew.

‘You,’ he said.

Reader, you don’t want to hear what I had to say to that.

# ACT III
# **CORPSING**

## SCENE FOURTEEN
## THE WINDMILLS OF MY MIND

*Friday May 7th. Midday.*

When we arrived at the rendezvous point, I was not at my best. It had been a rough old few days and I was beginning to feel the effects of all the beatings, bumps, scrapes, burnings and terrorisations. It had taken a lot to get me motivated that morning but Ms Agent Smith had come up with a cunning plan.

She got me off my tits on drugs.

I had surprised myself, given my somewhat distressed state, by falling asleep within seconds of touching the floor in the spare bedroom.

There was a bed in this one but I was too tired to walk that far.

I had woken unable to move most of my left side. My right side I could not move at all. Ms Agent Smith had come through and asked if I had any pain.

I laughed in her face. She looked me up and down and conceded it had been a stupid question. Almost every inch of my body was as black and swollen as a corpse. And kind of smelt like one too, even after a shower.

She told me I probably needed some kind of relaxant and so she gave me an injection of ketamine.

'Isn't that a horse sedative?' I asked

'Yes,' she replied, 'but I won't give you much.'

'Is that because I'm feeling a little *hoarse*?' Oh, how we laughed.

I told her I was too tired to move and felt as though my heart was about to stop beating. She gave me an injection of adrenaline. When I stopped bouncing off the walls I told her I was still in a great deal of pain, so she gave me morphine. That really spaced me out so she gave me some speed. As I was waiting for the full benefit of this pharmacopeia to kick in, I wondered out loud why she should have so many drugs just hanging around the place.

'My girlfriend,' she muttered.

'What, she's some kind of drug dealer?' I slurred. 'That must raise a few eyebrows, what with you being...'

'No,' she smiled, 'she's an army medic.'

'Ah,' I murmured, as the walls started to glow pretty colours and my teeth gritted like a Staffordshire terrier's around its favourite postman's leg. 'So she has all of this in case of some...national security crisis, then? Civil war in London. The Apocalypse.'

'No, she's a recovering addict and sometimes needs a little pick me up. How are you doing, now?'

I would have told her that I still didn't feel so good but I couldn't stop grinding my teeth. Just as well really. I might have told her about the hot flushes and the fact that my memory was going, and then she'd have thought I was menopausal and started me on a course of HRT.

Inspector Mallefant turned up in his shiny car and was carrying some fresh clothes for me to wear. Normal, clean clothes. And shiny brogues. And a tweed cap. I turned my nose up at the cravat, though. He still made me sit on a plastic sheet in the back, but to be fair he also made Ms Agent Smith sit on a plastic sheet on the driver's seat. She looked as though she was used to it.

We set off.

Ms Agent Smith had called Sam earlier and he had gone for it. She told him she had had to make a quick getaway to make sure that the children on the bus were safe, as well as Van G and Joshua, but that after dropping them off she had returned to the sewage works and found me creeping out of a manhole cover. He believed that she had single-handedly captured me, tied me up and dragged me back to her apartment where she had managed to contain me overnight. As if.

We were to meet them on the South Bank, near the London Eye, at just before midday. I glanced at my watch, realised I didn't have one (where had that gone?) and started singing 'The Windmills of My Mind'.

I just couldn't stop. On and on and on and on. Round and round. Like a wheel within a wheel. Like a circle in a circle. Ring within a ring. Hoop within a hoop.

Eventually Ms Agent Smith stopped the car, rolled a cigarette, slapped me on the head and said, 'Here, smoke this, it'll make you feel better.'

'Don't smoke!' I said. And then laughed at how absolutely hilarious her ears were. (Mind you, they were quite funny even when I wasn't on drugs. Don't ask me why, humour is a very personal thing.)

She slapped me again. 'You need to calm down. Smoke it!'

I smoked it. Three puffs in, I fell asleep. I dreamt we were walking along the South Bank, away from the Hungerford Bridge. We were headed towards the London Eye, which towered over us as we approached it.

'Like an eye within an eye...'

Sam was there and I told him he was a naughty American and that he should be ashamed of himself. He'd let himself down, he'd let his country down, he'd let the class down, he'd let my tyres down.

Everyone was talking at me, but I couldn't hear a word they were saying. Only the echoes of my…er…only see their mouths moving and a kind of *Wah! Wah! Waaaah!* sound coming out.

I stared up at the London Eye again. It stared back. I blinked first. Bugger.

'Like a cog within a cog...'

Mr Van G was there and asked if I would like a mint.

'Like a polo within a polo...'

'WILL-YOU-PULL-YOUR-SELF-TO-GETHER-AND-SHUT-THE-FUCK-UP!' said Joshua, suddenly appearing in his wheelchair within a wheelchair.

'Hello, Joshua,' I said, bending over to hug him. 'Ah Joshua, it's lovely to see you! How the devil are you, you creepy little bastard? By the way, did your voice thingummy come pre-programmed with "fuck" in it or did you have to add it yourself? Eh? Naughty Joshua! Who's a bad Joshua, eh?'

'UP-YOURS-ARSE-BISCUIT!' said Joshua.

I fell over laughing and I might have wee'd myself just a little bit at that.

Then some clowns were coming towards us. I jumped up and squeezed the nose of one of them, who said, 'Mr Rants this is hurting me. Letting me go, please. We are having your wifes here, as per what our bargaining was.'

I let go of his nose.

'It's you! Showaddywaddy!' I hugged and kissed them all. When I let them go they looked rather uncomfortable and embarrassed.

'What was it you were saying about my wife? You're shaving her hair, did you say? You want to be careful with that, she likes her hair a very lot much.'

People were staring at me as they walked past.

'What?' I shouted, with all the belligerence of a dormouse. 'I can make a noise if I want to. It's my dream! Now go away! I have to go and shave my wife with Showaddywaddy.'

Sam said, 'Mike, if you don't calm down I swear I'm going to knock you out.'

'Ha!' I said. 'Hahahahahahahahaha ha! You can't knock me out though can you? Because I'm asleep! And if you're not careful I will turn you into a…windmill! Like a floater in a toilet...like a something in your shoe...'

Sam knocked me out.

When I came to, I looked up and saw the face of Anna, smiling down at me.

'Hello, lovely man,' she said. 'You've come to rescue me. I knew you would.' And she bent forward and kissed me softly on the lips.

'Ooooh!' I said, 'I've died and gone to heaven. Hello, little angel.'

'God,' she said, 'you're not still using that cheesy old line, are you?

That went out with the dinosaurs. Did you remember to ring work for me?'

'Oh, bugger!' I said. 'I knew there was something. But what with trying to save your life and being tortured and blown off and all...'

'Blown off?'

'Up. I meant "up".'

'I hope you did. Well anyway, don't get all Mr Rant on me. I was only joking.'

She looked a bit teary.

'I'm sorry,' I said. And I was. A bit.

I felt a little less...excitable than I had before...before...

'He punched me!' I said.

'Who punched you, darling?'

I looked around and there stood Sam in...some kind of hamster cage?

'Wow, my dreams are getting weirder.'

'Mike, you're awake now.' She looked at Ms Agent Smith accusingly. 'My God, he is out of it. What did you give him?'

'Just some painkillers,' said Ms Agent Smith. 'And a bit of penicillin.'

'Maybe he's having an allergic reaction,' Anna said. 'Look at the colour of him!'

Ms Agent Smith knelt by my head and took my pulse. Her blonde hair shifted gently as she shook her head. She looked soft and caring, underneath those killers' eyes.

'He's fine,' said Ms Agent Smith. 'Just a little...overwrought. And that's just bruising you can see. He's had a rough few days.'

As she stood up and moved to join Sam in the hamster cage, I silently thanked her. Anna was staring at me.

'You haven't got something going on with her, have you?' she asked, bitterly. 'Because if you have...'

*Oh Anna,* I thought. *If you only knew. Yes she's beautiful, and kind of sexy in a Gestapo sort of way, but she's a lesbian. She wouldn't be interested in me.*

'So you did fancy her. I knew it! You always did like a woman in uniform.'

*Oops,* I thought. *Did I really say that out loud?*

'Yes you did.'

'Anna, I've spent the last few days desperately trying to find you. I've been to hell and back. And I even had to go to Birmingham. I've been so worried about you. Ask any of this lot. I'm just so glad that you're alright. You're the only woman I've ever wanted.'

Well, apart from a weird crush on Thora Hird when I was about eighteen.

'Thora Hird?'

'Stop it, Anna, you're freaking me out, reading my mind like that. Just hold me.'

And she did. A little stiffly at first, and then we folded into each other's arms and hugged hard. *I love you so much, you cantankerous old thing,* I thought.

'Who are you calling old?' she muttered into my shoulder. Then her hand reached down and gently caressed my balls.

'Ooh!' I said. 'Careful, darling. Little bit sensitive down there.'

I looked up and two members of Showaddywaddy were smiling down at me. One was dabbing his eyes with a tissue. The other gave me the thumbs up and I noticed the bandaged stump that had once been a finger.

'Is happy time for you, no?'

Anna pulled away. 'Oh, Mike, this is Stephan and Giorgio. They've been...looking after me.'

They nodded their hellos and I stared back at them.

*One false move and I'll kill the pair of you,* I thought.

'Mike!' said Anna. 'Be nice. They've treated me really well and if anyone is going to do any killing it'll be me. How could you get us into such a mess?'

'If you'd just let me explain...'

'Later. But it better be a good one.'

I sighed. The drugs were wearing off a bit and I realised this was no dream. Which was a good thing, because Anna was here and alive and well. But it was a bad thing for many of the same reasons. And I could murder a Mars Bar.

'I don't have a Mars Bar,' said Anna, rummaging through her bag, 'but I've got some custard creams in here somewhere.'

'Where are we anyway?'

'On the London Eye.' she said. 'I've wanted to go on for ages. We've missed a lot of it, you were out cold. Come and look at the view.'

I stood up stiffly and staggered to the window. We were about halfway down. As I looked around the gondola thingy I saw the Romanians lined up on the seats to one side, whilst Ms Agent Smith, Sam, Joshua and Mr Van G sat along the other. They all looked a bit grumpy.

Below us I could see police moving in amongst the crowd and moving them back. And in the distance I was sure I saw the bumbling figure of Special Constable Meads, directing the police cars where to park and looking decidedly happy. I turned back to the assembled company.

The suitcases were now on the Romanian side and a large briefcase was in Sam's hands. I had obviously missed the deal. Still, I had everything I wanted in my arms. If she had been holding the briefcase full of money it would have been the cherry on the cake, obviously, but still...

'I think you better stop now,' said Anna, a little harshly.

Don't do drugs, boys and girls. People can see your thoughts.

I looked around at the assembled company.

'Oh for God's sake, cheer up,' I said. 'You've all got what you wanted. The money, the disks. I have my lovely wife—'

'And child,' said Anna.

'I have my lovely wife and child back. Wow. Forgot about that for a second. Wow. That's amazing. You should all be happy. I'm the one who should be pissed off, I mean, Mallefant's going to have me arrested as soon as I step off this thing so...'

Oops.

Everyone was looking at me now. Apart from Ms Agent Smith who had closed her eyes and was muttering silently.

'The policeman?' asked Sam quietly. 'Are you telling me that miserable Scottish policeman is here?'

'What is miserable Scot-tish policeman?' Primary Romanian Goon asked. One of the sub-goons whispered in his ear and suddenly all of the Romanians had pulled out guns and were pointing them at the GIA.

'Keep calm, everyone.' I said. 'They're only after me. I'm the one who's been on a one-man crime spree across the country.'

Anna was staring at me, goggle-eyed.

'Sorry,' I corrected myself. 'I'm the one who has been on an *alleged* one-man crime spree across the country. Don't get your knickers in a twist. I'll go quietly and you lot can all disappear to wherever it is international criminals disappear to. Underground lairs? Secret island hideaways? Barnsley? Whatever. I just wanted the chance to see my lovely wife again before they lock me up and throw away the key.'

I hugged and kissed her and everyone looked to have relaxed a little. Stephan/Giorgio was dabbing at his eyes again.

The Romanians didn't put their guns away, though.

We were almost back at the disembarkation point. 'Well,' I said, 'it's been lovely knowing you all. I do hope your various nefarious fiendish plots all come to fruition. Not. But I think that my lovely wife and I will leave you now and spend our last few moments together. You all take care now.'

'I am think no,' said Primary Goon. 'What I feeling is, you and lovely wifes yours, will sit down now and maybe be have another turn around big wheel-thingy—'

'Did you learn your English from a bad English sitcoms of the eighties compilation DVD?' I wondered out loud.

'Quiet!' he screamed. 'No more the wise ass-cracking Mr Rants. You are sits here and we are go. We are being given head start. And I thinking also, we are make the penis...'

He looked doubtfully at his cohorts and spoke quietly in Romanian. They muttered back.

'...we are make the *penalty*. So we not payings for the goods. You give back now.'

'I don't think so, buddy,' said Sam.

'I think yes.'

He motioned to Giorgio/Stephan and he walked over and grabbed the handle of the briefcase. There was a brief tug of war and then Sam relented.

'You're going to be sorry for this,' he said.

*Hear, hear,* I thought, then realised Sam was talking to me.

'What? What did I do?'

'Limey idiot,' said Sam.

The doors hissed open and the Romanians started to back toward them.

Then a loud voice said, 'If youse don't mind, gentlemen. Ah think Ah'll tek they bags from you. Ah do believe they're the property of yon Secret Services.'

Hooray for Inspector Mallefant!

Then the Romanians turned their guns on him.

'Ah!' he said. 'Nae need tae be hasty the noo, gentlemen. Ah'll let youse be on yer way.' And he stepped to one side gingerly.

Boo to Inspector Mallefant!

Still, I sighed with relief as the Romanians backed slowly out of the door, smiling. It was over. Barbu was gone. I would never see the GIA again. I wouldn't have to worry about household bills where I was going. Though I would miss Anna terribly and wouldn't get to see my child growing up. And Anna would never get to see me grow up.

And now the Romanians were gone. Waving cheerfully as they escaped with the disks. And the money. Lots and lots and lots of money...

It was a moment of madness. I blame the drugs. As the doors began to close, I rushed forward and barged into the two Romanian henchmen holding the suitcases. Sam and Anna both shouted 'No! Mike, don't!' and I was touched by their concern. They *did* love me. Or Anna did. Sam obviously liked me a little bit more than he'd ever let on.

Right Hand Goon and Left Hand Goon fell like skittles, and I swiftly pirouetted and kicked Primary Goon right in the nuts. He hit a perfect high C and folded in half. I hefted up the two suitcases and was about to dive back through the door when I had second thoughts and scooped up the briefcase containing the cash with my toe and flicked it over my head into Anna's waiting arms. *Bend it like Beckham!* I thought. I was like a wild man on drugs. In fact I *was*...etc. etc.

I dived back through the narrowing gap with inches to spare – and stopped dead, falling over in a perfect pratfall onto my back. One of the suitcases had come through but the other was trapped in the door.

Primary Goon was staggering to his feet and advancing towards me, pulling a gun from his jacket as he did so. I yanked at the case but it wouldn't budge.

'Help me!' I shouted.

Anna and Ms Agent Smith both grabbed at the handle and pulled. For a second nothing happened and then it suddenly popped through and we all fell on our backs. Well, I fell on my back and Anna fell on hers. Ms Agent Smith fell on my front, and if I hadn't known better I would have sworn it was because she fancied me.

'Oh no you don't, lady. Climb off the hero, he's all mine.'

Anna threw Ms Agent Smith across the gondola and straddled me. God it was a turn on. It hurt like buggery but it was still a turn on.

'Take me now, big boy,' she said and cackled like a cackly thing that's just been tickled. I coughed and looked across at the others. Anna reluctantly climbed to her feet.

'Sorry,' she said to the assembly. Sam sat with his head in his hands and Inspector Mallefant had gone a charming shade of puce. 'Must be my hormones. Don't know what came over me. But I wish it had been you, you...big...brave...hunk of spunk!'

She pulled me to my feet and planted a kiss on me like a camel sucking a watermelon.

'Oh, get a room!' said Ms Agent Smith.

'BEEDLY-BEEDLY-BEEDLY!' said Joshua.

A phone was ringing. It was playing the theme from *Born Free*. Sam pulled it out of his pocket and answered with a somewhat tired, 'Hello?'

He listened for a moment and then held the phone out.

'It's for you,' he said.

I put the phone to my ear. It was our Romanian friend.

'Hahahahahaaaaaah, Mr Rants. How are youse enjoying your ride there? Ha ha ha! You are thinking haps that you are the winning, no? You are the money, you are the disks, and you are the wifes. All is good for you, yes?'

I moved to the window, still holding Anna tightly to my side, and looked down the ten feet or so to where the Romanian and his friends stood on the embankment. He was dancing like a pixie.

'But I am here telling you that it is no to you, Mr Rants. You are not the winning. Why? you might be asking. Why is no? Why is silly man say no? Are you asking? Asking me Mr Rants. I said to be asking!'

'Oh,' I said. 'Why?'

'Ha ha ha! Is very good question Mr Rants. And here for you is the bonus that is added. Enjoy your time wifes yours, because – be seeing clear what it is that I say – you will be having only the fifteen minutes there Mr Rants. After that, the ejaculate that I placed myself in the money bag will be spreading.'

There was some muttering in the background.

'Sorry, excusing Mr Rants. I say again – the ex-plosive I placed in the money bag will be blowing you. I am pressing button to start countdown now. Here we are going...and....boop! Is done. So is good bye to you and your friends Mr Rants. Love your wife good now. Can you see me here, Mr Rants? I am fingering you myself, Mr Rants! I am fingering you myself to you with the two fingers.'

I looked down, and he was indeed fingering me with two fingers.

'Goodbye Mr Rants. Goodbye*eeaiiieee*—!'

The last was a scream as three burly policemen rugby-tackled him to the ground.

I disconnected the call.

'What did he want?' asked Anna, brushing back my hair.

'Oh, nothing really,' I said. 'Do you really love me, Anna?'

'Of course I love you! Why do you even... Mike? What have you done now? Please tell me you haven't screwed up now. And you were doing so well. I was almost glad to see you. You have, haven't you? You knacker. Just tell me, what have you done?'

There were shots below us. We all rushed to the window and watched as the two Romanians were wounded and arrested. I craned my neck around and saw that three of the operators of the London Eye had also been wounded in the crossfire. The rest were running for their lives across the embankment. They disappeared into the crowd.

'What did he say, Mike?' said Sam, with a kind of halfway grin on his face. 'You may as well tell us.'

'Well,' I said, 'you see...the bag with the money in...sort of... has some...how do I put this? Well, explosives I suppose. And our Romanian friend just pressed the start button on a timer and don't look at me like that Anna, I wasn't to know! He says we have about fifteen minutes left before we—Ow! Anna, that hurts. I'm not a well man. Please! We have so little time left, let's not spend it fighting. I—*OOOOWW!!*'

'After you, Mrs Rant,' said Sam.

'Don't you start,' I said, trying to get Anna's fingers out of my hair and eyes.

'Well, I have to admit,' he said, 'that I am also a little to blame for our predicament.'

We both stopped and looked at him.

'What do you mean?' we asked in unison.

'Well, I did play the same little prank on our Romanian friends.'

'Meaning?' asked Ms Agent Smith.

'That I also planted explosives. In the case that I was giving to them. Purely to make sure that they didn't get away with material of national importance, you understand.'

'In the case that Mr Rant snatched back off them?'

'Indeed.'

Now Ms Agent Smith began to advance on me. 'God, you stupid f—'

Anna stepped in front of me. 'Oh, no! Step away from the gonk, lady. He's all mine.'

'What happened to "hero"?' I asked.

'If you search deep down inside yourself, I think you already know the answer to that question.'

She wasn't wrong.

'The windows,' said Van G. 'Try to break the bloody windows, and then we can throw the dashed things out!'

We tried. They were made of reinforced glass. We bashed them and kicked them, we hit them with the cases (which I pondered the wisdom of, given that they now had live bombs in them, but I really wasn't in any kind of position to question anybody else's moves). Ms Agent Smith even took a shot at one but the bullet ricocheted off and went pinging around until it found Van G's foot.

'Goodness gracious!' he said quietly. 'That smarts!' And then he fainted.

Ms Agent Smith sighed, pulled out her medicine pack, and set to work patching him up.

'Well,' I said to Anna. 'This is another fine mess I've gotten us into.'

And then I thought of the rubber masks that Sam and I had found under Willoughby-Chase's bed. I giggled. Looking across at Sam I saw that he'd had the same thought; we both snorted, then pursed our lips to try and stop. Sam failed and blew an enormous raspberry.

I howled.

'What the eff is wrong with you?' asked Anna. She looked so serious I couldn't help but honk another enormous, burping laugh in her face.

She snorted and then covered her mouth.

'You're bonkers, right. You do know that, don't you?'

'Get a grip,' said Ms Agent Smith. 'There's an injured man here.'

'Blow me!' said Sam, and hooted with glee.

She turned on him, about to have a go, and then her shoulders slumped and she puffed out a laugh. 'Ah, what the fuck,' she said. 'We're all going to be dead in a few minutes anyway.'

That stopped the laughter. We all stood silently, reminded that this was the end. We looked at each other guiltily and wiped our eyes.

Then Van G Sat bolt upright and said, 'I say, any chance of a sympathy shag from anyone? Not fussy, any port in a storm and all that. It's been a long time so you'll have to be patient with me...'

And we were off again. Creased up, thigh-slapping, barking mad laughter. We just couldn't stop. Even Joshua's voice box was saying HA-HA-HA-HA-HA over and over again, which set us off even more.

I pulled Anna to me and led her over to look at the view across the river. We giggled gently as we walked.

'I'm sorry, Anna. I—' she pressed a finger to my lips and then kissed me. Long seconds passed in the nicest way possible. I felt a stirring in my loins.

‘Enjoy the view with me, darling,’ she said, and laughed softly, turning her back and pushing her delectable bottom into my groin. In the window glass I saw the reflection of the tears running down her face. I cupped her precious tummy and tried not to howl. ‘We would have been great parents, wouldn’t we?’ I said.

‘The best,’ she said, and carried on gyrating her batty.

‘Oooh!’ I whispered. ‘Careful, darling. Still a little bit tender down there.’

We were almost at the top of the arc, and while we bumped and ground we took in the vista. The Houses of Parliament. Nelson’s Column. St Paul’s Cathedral. A helicopter floating over the river. Canary Wharf in the distance. The Oxo building. The bridges.

Behind us, Joshua had dismantled the housing of the electrical circuits in the wall of the pod and connected up the laptop of his computer. He was hacking the London Eye system, trying to open the doors so we could “eject our payload”, as he put it. All he seemed to succeed in doing was stopping the wheel and reversing it every thirty seconds, so we seemed to hover permanently at the top of the ride. I looked at the view again and held Anna a little tighter.

That helicopter was a lot bigger now.

And heading straight for us.

I thought it was going to crash straight into the Eye, but at the last second it banked and hovered right above us. Someone leant out of the door and began scouring the gondolas with a pair of binoculars. When they were looking straight at me, they were lowered. The man smiled. Waved.

Bela Barbu.

He put the binoculars down behind him and replaced them with an enormous rifle. *Uh-oh,* I thought.

'Everybody down on the floor, *now!*' I shouted, and pulled Anna away from the window.

They all dived and rolled under the seats just as a deafening crack filled the gondola. He must have been using some really big bullets. The glass in the roof cracked from side to side. He took aim again and this time the roof shattered and broken shards cascaded down on top of us.

Slowly the helicopter manoeuvred above us and a rope began to descend. I peeked up and saw Barbu thumbing a radio handset. His voice boomed out through the loudspeakers and echoed all around us.

'Good afternoon, ladies and gentlemen. I was worried I might have missed you. I do hope you're all enjoying the view. Now, you will see the rope that is descending towards you. I think you know what I would like you to do. So, as quickly as you can, please. Before I decide to start playing with my rifle again. You've seen the damage that that can do.'

I told Anna to stay where she was and she said, 'Too bloody right. This is your effing mess and you can effing well clear it up.' Ah, Anna. I do love you so.

Looking as dejected as it was possible to look, I crawled out from under the seat and held my hands up.

'Ah, Mr Rant! How lovely to make your acquaintance again. You are keeping your pecker up, I trust?'

I scowled up at him.

'Oh, don't be such a sore loser,' he said. 'Carry on, Mr Rant. Tie the suitcases on for me, there's a good chap.'

I tied them on and tried to hide the briefcase behind my back. I saw Eugene's face peer out through the door and he said something to Barbu.

‘Oh, I think we’ll have the money too, Mr Rant. We don’t want you profiting from your exploits. What kind of message would that send out to the young people of today?’

I fastened it on, flashed my middle finger at him, and retreated back under the seat.

‘Farewell all! I will be back, as all the best villains say. See you in your dreams.’

Slowly, the bags began to rise. *Come on,* I thought, *we must be down to the last dregs now. Hurry up, for fuck’s sake.*

The cases cleared the roof, and the helicopter began to bank over the river and away. Through the loudhailers we could hear Barbu singing:

‘If I were a rich man, biddy, biddy, biddy, biddy, biddy, biddy, biddy—’

BOOOOOOOOOOM!

Reader, I cheered.

## SCENE FIFTEEN
## STIR CRAZY

*Now*

I sit at the prison table. My hands are manacled to it, and my feet are manacled to the chair. I am only allowed visits from my wife (and anyone else, for that matter) under these conditions. I am considered a dangerous man. My life is spent in solitary, and I have been told this is as much for my own protection as for the protection of others.

The prison guards watch me openly, tauntingly.

Over the months my wife has come to regard me with increased suspicion, convinced that I am the homicidal maniac that everyone says I am. She has joined the ranks of friends and family who have slowly but surely become convinced of my guilt. I am the last person who believes that I am a falsely accused man. But I have a plan.

Today it will come to fruition.

Everything is in place. There is just one final cog to be placed within the mechanism and the machinery of justice will spring into action.

I giggle.

Someone tuts loudly.

'Sorry,' I say.

One must be so careful at these times. I am under surveillance at every moment. Their cameras recording my every tic, every lie, every truth.

But I can't help myself.

I giggle, I laugh, I guffaw, and pretty soon everyone around me is joining in.

The director walks onto the set and throws up his hands in exasperation.

'Okay, we'll cut there and take ten minutes out, everybody relax. And for pity's sake, Mike, pull yourself together.'

So everything worked out rather well. All things considered.

I feel I still have rather a lot to make up to Anna, but she is gradually coming round to the fact that I didn't do nearly as much wrong as she thought I had. Though I haven't told her the whole truth, of course.

The whole helicopter crash on the Thames/garage blowing up in Gloucestershire/Crimewatch hunt for Mike Rant was repackaged as a pre-publicity stunt for a new TV crime show called *Breakaway*, in which I am currently starring. The ratings are high, the intellectual level of the script is low. I do not expect it to stretch to another season.

Whilst I was still in the hospital recovering from general exhaustion and bodily (not to mention substance) abuse, under heavy police guard and the influence of what felt like more horse sedatives, I received a somewhat unexpected visitor.

I was dozing, in between police interviews and offers from the press for exorbitant amounts of money to tell "my side of the story", when a familiar voice said,

'Well now, here's a pretty picture. And how is Mr Stinky this fine morning?'

I was reaching for the bell to summon a nurse or a burly policeman, when Sam waved his hand at me. 'No point, Mike,' he said, 'I've sent them all on their way. Thought it might be nice to have a little quality time together.'

He sat on the edge of the bed and it creaked ominously as I rolled towards him.

'Seriously, Mikey boy,' he said, 'how are you doing?'

'What the hell are you doing here?' I managed. 'I would have thought you'd be as far away from here as possible, raking in the cash from your ill-gotten gains and conning the teeth out of your Granny's head. And you can quit with the phoney American accent, it's really not that good anyway.'

He smiled.

'What have you got to smile about?' I spluttered. 'Apart from being very rich and having the governments of several countries in your pocket, I mean. You know they'll shoot you dead if they catch you round here. And probably me as well while they're at it, so bugger off and be smug in someone else's bedroom.'

He just looked at me for a long time, then said, 'You don't believe everything you read on the internet, do you Mike?'

'What do you mean?'

He considers for a few seconds. Then, 'Let's say, just for argument's sake, that a certain businessman got hold of some highly inflammatory material regarding certain highly placed individuals. And that said businessman was using said material to influence…affairs of state.'

'Okay,' I said, 'you've said it. Now fu—'

'Let's say as well that certain government departments got wind of this and wanted to eradicate the problem. Now, whilst it's all very well giving such an order, certain officials might want to put a little… distance…between themselves and the solution to their problems. Do you follow?'

'No,' I said, though I was beginning to.

He sighed. 'See, it's all about necessary evils, Mr Rant. The balance of power. There is a problem, and there is a solution. But both must be kept at arm's length, lest anyone find out what is going on. They are intertwined. Admit to members of the CIA acting on British soil to eradicate foreign nationals and the threat they represent, and you have, at least to a degree, to confess that there was a threat.'

My head is spinning, but one thing is becoming clear.

'Are you trying to tell me,' I said slowly, 'that the whole thing about you being a gangster was a bluff? That you really are a member of the CIA or something?'

'I couldn't possibly confirm or deny any such thing.'

'Oh, for Christ's sake!' My head felt like it was going to burst. 'What happened? Who are you? Who the hell won this battle?'

'The good guys.'

'The theoretical good guys, who might or might not exist and will, theoretically at least, kill me if I try to prove it one way or the other and who will happily see me banged up in order to cover their tracks?'

'Something along those lines. But it needn't come to that.'

'What do you mean?'

He opens the briefcase he is carrying and pulls out a formal looking document. He flicks over a few pages and then hands it to me, along with a cheap disposable pen.

'If you could just see your way to signing this.'

'What is it?'

'Let's just say that it may or may not be a copy of the Official Secrets Act. Along with authorisation for you to act on behalf of the American Government in order to protect British soil from foreign incursion.'

'You mean…you're signing me up as a spy?'

'Oh, I couldn't—'

'—possibly comment. Yeah, yeah. Give me the pen.'

I signed, and then started riffling through the pile of papers, but he whipped them away from me, folded them and shoved them into his jacket pocket.

'Of course, you may have just signed a confession to all of the things you've been accused of in the last few days. And believe me, should push come to shove, your signature will find its way onto just such a document. And do bear in mind that no bodies were recovered from the wreckage of the helicopter pulled from the Thames. I'm sure you wouldn't want Mr Barbu or his associates to suddenly come into possession of information as to your whereabouts. Because if they did you might require a little more protection than you or your good lady wife could muster.'

'You fat Yankee bastard.'

'Sweet talker. For now then, Mr Rant.' He wiggled his fingers at me in farewell and turned to go.

'Just tell me one thing,' I say to his back.

He does not turn. 'If I can,' he says.

'Are you one of the good guys, or one of the bad guys?'

He turned back to me and sighed.

'It's a complicated world, Mr Rant. Sometimes people do the right thing for the wrong reasons. Or the wrong thing for the right reasons. Or any other combination you care to come up with. In your case I'd go for...doing the wrong thing for all the wrong reasons and yet still coming out okay, ish.'

'Is that an answer or did you just open a fortune cookie?'

He paused.

'Let me put it this way. If I work for the government and some of my work is somewhat…beyond the normal realms of legality, I wouldn't be likely to tell you, now would I? And if I'm a gangster, and my business practices have the blessing of several governments, either willingly or unwittingly – well, I wouldn't be likely to tell you that either, now would I?'

'No,' I said.

It wasn't that I understood what he was telling me; it just felt like he was waiting for me to say something.

'Just be glad that we won this one, Mike. You've seen the contents of those disks, and nobody in their right mind is going to prosecute you for your part in proceedings. Because we, whoever we are, will make sure that that will not happen. And if it does, you'll be dead before your feet hit the courtroom floor. So, good guys or bad guys, you're one of us now. Remember that, because we will.'

He let that sink in.

'Maybe we'll call on you again. One day.'

I opened my mouth, and then closed it.

'What?' he asked.

'I was going to say I'd rather be dead. But there's a good chance they'd amount to the same thing, if this week has been anything to go by.'

He smiled.

'Ciao, Mike. Take good care of yourself. And keep fighting the good fight.'

He had almost closed the door when he stopped, reopened it and looked at me with a smile.

'Oh, yes,' he said. 'Silly me. Almost forgot.'

He walked back over to the bed and handed me the briefcase.

'Is this a bomb?' I asked as he walked away.

'That rather depends on your point of view, doesn't it?' he said, and closed the door behind him.

I clicked back the catches.

Opened the case.

Stared at the bundles of cash sitting there. I knew without counting that it would come to a total of one hundred thousand English pounds.

Less expenses.

And sixty-four pence for a bottle of milk.

On top of the notes was a plain white envelope.

On the envelope was written:

*Thought this might come in useful.*
*Use it wisely,*
*S.*

It contained an unmarked DVD. *Hmmmm,* I thought.

So, theoretically at least, I am now a spy. A spook. I like to compare myself to Jack Bauer in *24*, though Anna tells me I am more like Jack

Duckworth in *Coronation Street*. They pay me a retainer, which does look kosher, directly into my bank account, in case they should ever want to call on my services again – or because they want to keep me quiet. I got terribly excited and couldn't wait to brag about it to all of my friends. But then Sam called one afternoon and told me that of course, I wasn't allowed to mention it. It appears on my accounts as having been paid by WH Smith.

I consoled myself with the thought of jetting off to far-flung corners of the world to fight evil, flirting with beautiful women, *no, of course I would never sleep with them, Anna,* and of never having to work again with my private income.

Then I found out that the retainer amounted to the princely sum of $100.00 US per year. Less tax.

'Did you ever,' I asked Anna one afternoon, while she was visiting me in hospital, 'did you ever in your wildest dreams imagine I would one day work for the CIA?'

'Babe,' she said, 'I'm sorry to tell you that you're not in my wildest dreams.'

And she fell quiet, with a dreamy look on her face.

For once, I didn't say anything.

And, of course, I now have a child. He is beautiful and it makes my heart glow every time I look at him, to think that I could have been a part of creating something so delicate, so wonderful, and so precious.

He is a symbol of all that is good between Anna and me, all of our dreams and aspirations, and how we feel toward one another.

Anna insisted that we call him Giorgio.

And that disk.

I know you're wondering.

Let's just say that it's amazing how many high up members of the media – television, stage, and screen – you can fit onto one small computer disk, all of them committing…well, let's just call them errors of judgement, large or small.

Of course I use it sparingly, and quietly.

And I would like to think that I succeeded in getting the lead role in *Breakaway* purely on the basis of my superior acting skills. But I don't think I'm kidding myself, let alone anyone else.

# EPILOGUE

*Inspector Mallefant is a happy man.*

*It has taken him some little while to realise this, as the feeling is so unfamiliar to him. He has brought a case to a conclusion, even though it is a conclusion that the public cannot get its grubby little paws on.*

*He sits behind his clean, sweet-smelling desk, where he spends most of his days now, and smiles to himself. He can choose the jobs he undertakes. He can set his own agenda. He is one of the invisible, sparkling, well-oiled cogs, which keeps the great machine of this country running.*

*He does occasionally take on outside work. He does sometimes even leave his office. But only for nice jobs. Clean jobs. A high-profile gala dinner for the glitterati, perhaps. Providing security at movie previews. Seeing a wealthy foreign diplomat safely onto his plane.*

*No one questions this, nobody complains. Hardly anyone even knows. Inspector Mallefant is his own man now, left to himself and largely ignored, which is just the way he likes it. Because Inspector Mallefant had had a chance to review the contents of the discs before they were hurriedly removed to some top secret bunker in a far-flung corner of Chingford or Hammersmith.*

*What he saw appalled him, shocked him and disgusted him. Especially the ones revealing the secret lives and fantasies of the Commanders and Chiefs of the British Constabulary. Almost every rank seemed to have been represented, but it was the top brass that saddened him most. And it was with a heavy heart that he made several copies and secreted them in places that even dirt could not penetrate. It was with a feeling of deep remorse that he wrote to all of those represented and advised them of their moral waywardness. And it was with regret that he accepted their fawning, wheedling and cajoling – and became the policeman he had always wished to be.*

*Little by little, hour by hour, day by day, Inspector Mallefant has begun to learn to love filth.*

*Look at him now.*

*A gathering of the great and the good from the media world, gathering to pat each other's back in the beautiful environs of Edinburgh's Plaza Hotel. Not the most morally enlightened people in the world, but their organisers have good taste. Beautiful food, beautiful surroundings, beautiful people – to the naked eye, anyway.*

*The problems he must surmount are small a price to pay for the peace, financial rewards and sanitary conditions he now enjoys.*

*Take this moment, for instance. There is a kerfuffle in the lobby;*

*someone has probably imbibed a little too much champagne with lunch. He wanders over to have a quiet word. If this does not work, then a simple nod will bring security down on them like the hand of God.*

*He is beginning to step through the crowd when he hears a familiar voice that chills him to the bone.*

*An excited voice.*

*A Northern voice.*

*He fights the urge to run away as the voice intones:*

*'Will you please for fuck's sake just let me explain!'*

## ACKNOWLEDGEMENTS

Writing a novel is a strange and drawn out undertaking. It can be a solitary and lonely journey, but also one full of joy and sharing. Over the years, many people get sucked in, used and abused, and very rarely properly thanked. Just like in Mike's world, I suppose. The following is far from an exhaustive list, but if I have missed you off, then I will say thank you, wholeheartedly. I'm sure you know who you are. Thanks to all of those who have read and suffered through various drafts of Rant with me, most especially Jeff Price and Lynda Price, Jacqui Wood (who'd have thought after all these years...?) and Andrew Wood. And to all of those who have made supportive noises about a hidden talent and kept me on the somewhat winding and convoluted track that led to there from here. Not least Linda Fitzsimmons. If anyone is likely to recognise Mike Rant, then she is. Thanks to all at Moth Publishing and New Writing North, especially Sarah Porter, Andrea Murphy, Claire Malcolm and Olivia Chapman for guiding me through the final stages and selecting me as one of the writers from the Northern Crime Competition. If I miss anyone off here, it is only because I don't know your name yet. Thanks also to you, gentle reader. Without you... And of course, last but definitely most, much love and thanks to my wife Kate Fox, who has shared her amber room with me for the last five years. Her reading, critiquing and laughter has helped and supported me through the difficult gestation and labour that has given birth to this somewhat strange and ugly child. I know that she would rather have had a puppy. If you want to keep up to date with Mike Rant, then you can Friend him on Facebook, follow him on Twitter, or read his on-going blog at rantability.blogspot.com Bye for now.